Season Of Waiting

By
Melanie Maniver

Order this book online at www.trafford.com
or email orders@trafford.com

Most Trafford titles are also available at major online book retailers.

Any resemblance to anyone living or dead is coincidental, but the Depression was real, and
the telling of it is my own.   MM

Note for Librarians: A cataloguing record for this book is available from Library
and Archives Canada at www.collectionscanada.ca/amicus/index-e.html

Printed in Victoria, BC, Canada.

ISBN: 978-1-4269-1633-5 (sc)
ISBN: 978-1-4269-1634-2 (dj)

Library of Congress Control Number: 2009934467

*Our mission is to efficiently provide the world's finest, most comprehensive book publishing
service, enabling every author to experience success. To find out how to publish your
book, your way, and have it available worldwide, visit us online at www.trafford.com*

Trafford rev. 02/22/2010

 www.trafford.com

North America & international
toll-free: 1 888 232 4444 (USA & Canada)
phone: 250 383 6864 ♦ fax: 812 355 4082

Any resemblance to anyone living or dead is coincidental, but the Depression was real, and the telling of it is my own.

–MM

Acknowledgements

People have asked me through the years when I was going to write another book. I didn't think about it until I realized I did have another one in the back of my mind, and one day I started writing and didn't quit. It is odd how once you get pen in hand, you don't want to quit. Most of my writing comes from either having lived it, witnessed it or just using a little imagination to make it come together.

Anyway, when I finished the last page, I had the most astounding thing to happen - - I had a heart attack. That heart surgeon must have done a good job, because I'm still here and praising the Lord first and the doctor second.

"Season of Waiting" is my way of presenting family values and the truths of human relationships that really mean something. Life is not always fair but hanging on to the right choices does matter after all is said and done.

Computers are amazing, and Laurie Metcalfe, Martha Denny, Kay Ford and Henry have all helped me get this book together and in print. Thank you.

You readers. Think about it. The last season of the years of your life may be amazing. I hope so!!

MM

Chapter 1

*S*pringtime had finally arrived in full glory, and Sissie and Jean were taking a long walk mostly so they could talk. Both girls were pretty in different ways. Jean was blond all the way, bright blond hair, blue eyes and even blond eyebrows. She was a little taller than Sissie and bigger boned, full bust'd and wider-hipped. She was attractive, to say the least, and she was dating the most sought-after guy in high school, Sissie was smaller, with brown-red hair down past her shoulders, graceful and completely feminine - -slender and beautifully put together – or so she had been told many times.

The two girls walked slowly down Lamar Street, circling the huge oak tree in the middle of the sidewalk "You know, Jean, Daddy told me that the Union soldiers camped around this tree during the War. I guess they rested after they burned most everything in town. Daddy said that Miss Maggie told him how her Grandmomma came out of what was left of her house and cussed them out, but they just laughed at her," Sissie looked back at the huge tree as they walked on down toward the Square. Jean was already thinking about the evening activities.

"Sissie, how about Freddie and I getting you a date tonight? We always have fun, and he knows a lot of guys who'd love to double date." Jean reached over and caught her friend's arm. "You stay home too much. There are lot'sa fellas coming to the Campus for this War, and here you are talking about the old War. Freddie likes you, but he says you're too smart for your britches." Jean laughed as she said this. Sissie gave her a hard look, and then they both smiled.

They had reached the Square, and they turned right toward the drug store. They both had a dime for an ice cream cone with two dips, and after they sat down on the counter stools, Sissie watched Jean as she slowly licked the ice cream, relishing every bit. She had always admired Jean's ability to accept every situation and make the best of it, but Sissie often thought of Jean's home situation being less than most. Sissie liked Jean's looks—her bright naturally blond hair, blue-blue eyes and full mouth. She was built well too, fuller-bosom'd than most of the girls in the tenth grade.

Several boys walked in, and two of them came over to the counter where they were sitting. Jean smiled and welcomed them casually, and they sat down. It was so easy for Jean , Sissie thought, and most of the conversation was hers with them. Sissie felt uncomfortable, and why she did not know. She didn't think about it right then, but later at home she felt let-down and unattractive. Casual conversation was something she could not manage, and she wished she could. In many ways she had much more than Jean, but in the ways that mattered to tenth graders, Jean had it all over her. My house is better, but I'm not. My Dad is great, my grades are better, we have a servant, and I shouldn't feel so rotten. She felt totally inadequate and was glad when they finished and left the boys still at the counter. They continued on their walk. "Say, look at this diamond ring in Stayler's window. That's the size I want when Freddie and I get married." Jean stared at the diamond until Sissie pulled her away.

It was July and Saturday, and the town square was full of wagons piled high with watermelons. There was not an empty space next to the Courthouse and few in front of the stores circling the Square. There was no air stirring, and the mules were stomping and shaking the flies away. The farmers brought their wares in on Saturday and spent the day lolling under the trees bordering the Courthouse lawn. Sissie stopped at Nalton's, the only department store in town. "let's go in—it's a little cooler in there," she said to her friend. They went in.

"Good gracious, Jean, look at the prices of these blouses— nearly four dollars! I'd love to have one, but I could never pay that price—wonder who could? " Sissie looked longingly at the perfume counter while Jean focused on the make-up. Both girls knew they could not buy anything, but it didn't cost anything to look. Nalton's Department Store was owned by the wealthiest family in Oakville, and Nancy Dalton was amazingly unaware of it, Nancy lived in the biggest house in town. It even had an iron fence around the five-acre front yard, and a movie was to be filmed in her home before too long. Nancy was not pretty and she knew it, but she also knew how to remember that she was in need of friends; and she really tried hard to make buddies like some of the other girls did. Sometimes she even wished she could be more like all the other girls her age and be better liked and have a boyfriend. That was her greatest wish. About the time Jean and Sissie were leaving the store, she saw them and waved. They waved back but walked on. Nancy tried to catch up, but they never looked back. Four years later, Nancy married Sam Tomas, handsome, but poor. It seemed a good match. Nancy and Sissie were to become good friends. Sam was to manage Nalton's Department Store.

Chapter 2

Oakville was a pretty little town, if "pretty" means big oak trees lining the two main streets, and clean, mowed yards. One could walk in any direction from the Square and not see any litter. The houses mostly sat way back from the asphalt streets, and the town limits meant gravel roads but still mowed and clean. Times were still hard in the early 1940's and Jean's Mother, Lula Belle, had finally gotten a job at the Bus Station selling tickets. Jean's sister, Mary, helped in the Science Lab at school and received a small fee. Her brother, Lucas, mowed lawns and did odd jobs. Jean's Dad had met a younger woman in an adjoining town three years before and had walked out one day and did not return. Lula loved that man, and she never really gave him up. Not too long afterwards he had an automobile accident which blinded him and his young wife couldn't take it. She walked out on him. Lula Belle took him back to her small lodgings and cared for him until his death. She had an easier time forgiving him than their three children did. They never referred to him again as "Dad" but called him by his first name. Lula reminded them that he was their father, but they could not forget as she had seemed to have forgiven as well as forgotten. The three rooms they had grown up in were reminders of his failure as a father, but they loved and respected their Mother enough to tacitly accept him back.

Jean and Sissie continued on in their walk, but soon the midday heat set in and they made their way toward home. The afternoon was already planned—the University swimming pool.

The football recruits were lined up at the fence around the swimming pool, and all were big, bronze giants. One of them was huge—reddish brown hair and blue eyes. When he smiled at the girls coming toward them, Sissie's heart skipped a beat. He looks like Rex Barker, the movie star, she thought, Bea Denton had managed to get her family car and had picked them up.

The three girls went in, paid their dime, and went into the dressing room. Bea could hardly wait to get outside and the other two followed shortly. She had already cornered the only one Sissie had noticed, so Sissie got on in the water and looked as indifferent as she could. One of the other guys came up behind her and picked her completely up and threw her into the twelve foot water. Sissie was a poor swimmer and fortunately Jean saw her. "Rex Barker" as later she jokingly called him sometimes, jumped in and pulled her to the side of the pool where she sputtered and tried her best to quit gasping for breath. He asked her if she was O.K. and turned to her agitator. "You better never do anything like that again. She could'a drowned - - slipping up on her that way." Sissie was embarrassed and sat on the edge of the pool for a minute before thanking him. He does look like Rex Barker, she thought, and he saved my life. The remainder of the summer she saw Herb several nights a week. He only kissed her once, and she was to never forget that kiss. Herb left the University that fall and joined the Marines. He was killed in the Pacific Theater. Some of us leave no mark in this world. Herb did. Sissie carried his memory through the many decades she lived. He was as alive to her as the first time she saw him standing at the fence that day; her heart never let him go. She felt that she would never feel that way again about anyone and for a very long time she cried herself to sleep at night. He was so wonderful, so big and handsome - - and so sweet. She had learned from one of his friends that Herb had been raised by his Grandmother who lived on a farm in Tennessee. She made a promise to herself that some day she would go and talk about him to someone else who loved him. She was to never fulfill that promise, as his Grandmother died only a few months after Herb was killed.

The summer wore on slowly, and it was time to return to the big old school building, hot and worn, but so welcome. Sissie loved school. She loved Latin, and she went to State Field Meet in American History and even Civics wasn't too bad. English and Literature were a breeze, and Mrs. Lackey approached her about editing the school paper the next year. Sissie had already made up her mind to go to summer school and finish a year early. The sooner she could get a job, the better. She thought about her home situation. There was no resentment because she knew that her father was doing all he could do to feed and clothe them. A family in need of something kept her father flat broke most of the time. The acceptable part of it was just about everybody else was in the same boat, and most were in worse shape than her family. Her older brother, Richard, was already in his fourth year at the University, and he had more demands than the other four - - out of necessity, he said. He lived in the Frat house but edited the College paper and paid some of his own expenses. Sissie was really proud of him, as he was elected to the Hall of Fame and went on to be outstanding in Law School. Her older sister, Evelyn, sang with the University orchestra, and they had summer engagements; so she managed to buy her own evening gowns and even managed to pay her own tuition. Sissie felt a complete stranger to her, as she never was home except when she had a date; and she knew that most of the time Evelyn forgot that she even existed.

Laney was only three years older than Sissie, and she was a real "tom-boy"—as Daddy called her. Up to lately, she played baseball with the neighborhood boys, shot rubber guns in the old barn across the street at the Alvin place, and usually had her pockets full of marbles which she won regularly from the guys who would shoot with her. She was stronger and could run faster than anyone around, and she didn't mind mowing the yard with the ancient mower, 'cause she said it kept her muscles in shape. Daddy kinda worried about her, thought Sissie, but as it turned out she got to be real pretty and she began to look at the boys as admirers rather than victims.

Bo was the youngest. He was only two when their Mother died. The doctor never told them what was wrong with her. The fact was he didn't know. In the early 30's and 40's that often happened. Sparse equipment and little funds to run the hospital made it difficult to find capable doctors and nurses, and the one doctor at the main hospital in town did the best he could under the circumstances. He had no X-ray equipment and never had time to up-date his medical knowledge. Her Mother had died at 37 years old, still beautiful but quietly accepting an ugly death. It almost seemed that she didn't care about living any longer and accepted death as inevitable. She was in constant pain, and Calvin Walker did not take the children to see her in that hot little room at the hospital; so her death was not as close to them as it should have been. When Sissie thought about it years later, she wondered why her father kept them away from their Mother as she lay dying. He was a kind and gentle man, but his reasons were his alone. He seldom shared them with his five children.

Chapter 3

*I*t was several years before he started seeing Sally Dunstan. She had begun working for the photographer in the office next to Calvin's, and she made a point to be around whenever he came in to talk to his friend, Lester Caulfield. Lester was always suggesting someone for him to see, and he had finally found someone. He and his wife asked them over to dinner, and Calvin surprised them and accepted. He began seeing Sally regularly outside the office and needless to say, his children resented it. Why, Sissie did not know, except Sally Dunstan had two big boys. That was enough for small town talk. Too, Sally was an outsider. She had appeared in Oakville the year before with no husband and never seemed to confide in her past with anyone. Lester Caulfield had hired her because she was pleasant and knew something about developing pictures and keeping his files straight. Also, Sally worked for less than he had paid before, and he liked her.

As Sissie thought about her and her Dad seeing her more and more lately, she began to watch Sally, furtively but constantly. Her father needed an assistant in his dental office, and Lester Caulfield was willing to let her change jobs for several reasons - - first and foremost - - he wanted to encourage Calvin to seek companionship - - and he thought Sally would fill the need.

Lester's wife, Maxie, liked them both, and she was a willing accomplice. Sissie began to be a regular visitor in her Dad's office, as the others, even Richard didn't seem to notice or care. Only once did she venture to talk to her father about his "love life" and in later years she was ashamed of her lack of respect and knowledge. Calvin Walker had been alone for a very long time, and he had begun to hate his life working eight to ten hours a day, answering calls even on Sunday, keeping five kids clothed and fed and paying for house help, laundry help and hands on his farm forever asking for something. Sally Dunston was a godsend. The depression was still in sway across much of the Nation, especially in the South, and even the very ground seemed to suffer. The crops on the farm were stricken with the lack of rain. Many times he lay awake at night wondering how he could cope with it all. The kids had no idea how strapped he was for cash, and more than that, how strapped he was for some joy in his life. Never once, though, did he say anything to his children when he saw them at the dinner table. Then and then only did he see them. Pearl, the black cook, always fixed the main meal at noon, and in order to be properly filled, the five children made sure they were there. The other meals they fended mostly for themselves. Usually, there were a few leftovers in the warmer above the stove. When Calvin came home at night, he would fix himself a glass of buttermilk with a piece of Pearl's cornbread in it. Peanut butter and milk was always available and sometimes fruit. They never went hungry as some did in Oakville. Calvin's dental patients seldom had any money, but they brought watermelons, turnip greens, cantaloupes and whatever their gardens produced. Most everyone had a garden, some chickens and a cow. A few had pigs which they butchered in the fall, and the Walker family often had ribs and chops for Sunday dinner. Bad as times were, few went hungry because they had to provide for themselves, and they managed. Pearl's husband, Ben, lived in a small frame house on five acres of land a short mile out of Oakville. He always had food for his grandchildren and himself, and Pearl usually would bring extra's when she came home. Dr. Walker had provided her a small house in the back of his home, and Pearl loved being there. It was quiet, she kept it clean, and it was all her own. Ben's brood was not hers, and she went to see him only for a day or two to help him catch up on the housecleaning and chores. She used the small salary she made to provide clothes and necessities for herself and Ben. The grandchildren Ben had to provide for, and he managed to keep them clothed and fed adequately. His small farm brought a little income, and the mother of the kids provided a little now and then. Ben called her "my sorry daughter". She was not Pearl's child, and Pearl had to really soul-search to accept her at all. Pearl did cook for the three boys when she went home and patched and cleaned their clothes. They were always glad to see her, and Ben would settle into his old rocking chair and relish her presence. Ben was a big man, muscular and handsome in his way. He still had broad shoulders and a flat belly, and though much darker than Pearl, he was popular with the ladies. He often wished he were "higher" color like his beloved Pearl. Pearl was the love of his life, but he could not be faithful to save his life. One of the kids in the house was proof of that, and he accepted the fact of his unfaithfulness with greater love and respect for his wife. Ben took charge of the children and provided for them as best he could, they never went hungry.

Dr. Walker had dropped Pearl off early on Sunday as he had been invited to the Sander's in Toccoco, not far from Oakville for dinner. All the other children had other plans, and he was glad to get away for the day. Pearl was received with much excitement, and she proceeded to look in the little ice box to see what she could fix for dinner. Like in the Walker home, they had dinner at noon, supper at night. There were fresh turnip greens washed and ready to cook, pole beans to snap, and corn still fresh on the cob. She had brought a big sack of cookies she had made the night before.

"Ben, there is no milk in for the cornbread," Pearl told her husband. He got up and started out the door.

"Well, ole Clarabelle is waiting right outside. It will only take a few minutes."

Pearl got the vegetables on the wood stove, stoking it, and asking the boys to fetch kindlin' from outside. They grinned and ran outside the door.

It was a while later when Ben came back in and the meal was almost ready. He sat the milk bucket down without a word and Pearl looked as he limped away. The bucket was less than half full.

"What happened to you, Ben?" The boys were snickering, and Ben glared at them.

"That dadburned cow stepped on my foot, and when I tried to get her off me she kicked the bucket over and splashed milk all over me. She knew it wasn't milkin' time." Pearl's shoulders were shaking and three pairs of white teeth were showing across the room. He turned to leave.

"Hurry up and get on something else, dinner will be ready in a few minutes," and Pearl turned away and tried hard not to laugh out loud.

When Ben returned a few minutes later, he had on some socks and no shoes; and he had changed into his other pair of overalls and a clean shirt. The boys sat at the table waiting for big Pearl as they called her to say the blessing. When she said "Amen" three pairs of arms reached for the hot cornbread and butter.

"Hold on a minute, boys," Ben bellowed. Since my big toe is hurtin' so bad, L.D. will take over the milkin' for a time, and you, James, will hoe out the garden come sun up. And you, Lester, will pick the beans. All of you startin' first thing in the morning."

L.D. quit grinnin' real fast, but the prospect of 5 o'clock in the morning didn't dim his appetite at all.

Chapter 4

*B*en had acquired a huge broad-breast bronzed turkey, with the stipulation that he was not to be eaten, but to prize him for his special talent – watch guarding property. He came with the name "Preacher Man", and he took his talent very seriously. In fact, Ben had to take a broom out with him for the first few weeks that Preacher Man had joined the family. Ben taught him some manners, but only as far as he, Ben, was concerned.

The first time Ben witnessed Preacher's special talent was when his best friend's wife drove out with a small table that she needed fixed. Ben was a pretty good fixer and his best friend was not. When she opened the door of the car, got out and bent back into the car to get the small table out, Preacher Man did his straight up jump and landed on her back. Preacher weighted around 30 pounds, so he gave her a real jolt as well as doing her only coat a good bit of damage. Being a country gal, she got in a few good licks before she got Preacher off her back. Ben thought it was funny, which made her even madder. She threatened to kill that big buzzard if he ever did that again.

Preacher Man almost ended any visitation to Ben's small farm, and Ben got real fond of the big turkey. He wasn't eager to have a lot of company, but when Pearl was due, Preacher Man got locked in the big wire cage in the backyard.

Ben's half-brother lived down the road from him, and J.C. was the middle son in the half-brother's family. One day J.C. decided to pay a visit to Ben's house, forgetting about the watch guard. Preacher Man stayed around the corner of the house until J. C. got close. He charged with his feathers spread like an umbrella. He jumped straight up and hit J.C. in the chest. It almost knocked the breath out of J.C., and he fell backwards hitting his head pretty hard. Preacher Man was getting ready for his second assault when J.C. decided to take off. Preacher ran him down to the road.

"You big buzzard, I'll get you back. You wait and see." J.C. was unwilling to tell anyone that a turkey had knocked him down and chased him home, but he planned his revenge.

His best friend had a dog that he included in his plan. He would take old Jag and sick him on that big buzzard and let him teach him a real lesson. The next morning J.C. and Jag walked slowly down the road, and it was almost that Preacher Man was expecting them. When they got halfway up the driveway, there he was waiting, his feathers puffed up like crazy. Jag looked a little leery, but J.C. said "Get 'em Jag," and he did. Preacher jumped straight up and landed on Jag's back and scratched, gobbled and pecked everywhere he could reach, and Jag couldn't seem to dismount him. It wasn't a pretty sight.

Jag finally dumped him but he had all he could take for one day, and he beat J.C. down the driveway and headed for home.

This would have been a fine story to pass around, but J.C. decided not to discuss it. He didn't want to ruin Jag's reputation.

Sad to say, but Preacher Man finally met his match when two

chow mixtures got loose and visited Ben's place. They ended the best turkey watch guard in the South that day, but Preacher died with great pride in his work. Both of those dogs went home with lifetime scars on their backs. It wasn't a victory that any dog would be proud of.

Chapter 5

*S*issie heard the horse hooves clopping down the blacktop, and she knew before she saw him and his beautiful horse who it was. He never called. He just showed up. She was bored and lonely as on most July days, and she got up from the swing on the big front porch. "Hi, Chris, come on up and join me. You and Pilgrim are out on a hot day." Christopher Fellner was a fine looking boy of seventeen and an ardent but diffident admirer of Sissie's. Last Valentine's Day at school he had brought eighteen Valentines to school to the Valentine party and all eighteen were for Sissie; otherwise, he paid her only a little attention at school.

"Come on, Sissie, and ride with me. You can sit behind me and hold on. Pilgrim needs the exercise." He fully expected her to refuse, but Sissie had on some pedal pushers and was ready to go. He dismounted and helped her up, and climbed onto the big saddle again. They clopped back up North Elm Street, across the Square and on to South Elm.

"Let's go to my house. I want to show you my new addition on the barn. My Step-dad said he's going to buy another horse so we can ride together." They chatted as they rode and soon turned into a long grassy entrance between huge trees lining each side. The two-story Colonial style house sat a way back, stately, old and somewhat in need of paint, but still proudly inviting.

They dismounted at the side, and Chris tied Pilgrim to a railing and they went in the front door. "Let's get a drink before we go out back," Chris said, and they walked down the hall, past the open doors on each side. On the right wall before they entered the kitchen was a small table with the phone. What attracted Sissie's attention was the handwriting on the painted wall.

"Your Step-dad must be writing another book," she said. "Does he always write it on the wall? Can I read it?"

"Sure," Chris answered. He handed her a glass of iced tea, and Sissie sat on the small chair and read some of the notes. They were disconnected and difficult to read, so she joined Chris and they went on back to see his new stalls and Pilgrim's special place. They sat on a bench and talked and finished their tea when a big old convertible pulled in the driveway. Chris took the glasses and set them in the window sill.

"We'd better go," he said. "I need to get you home before dark." They rode quieter than they had ridden earlier. And she thanked Chris for the ride. He said he'd see her again.

Sissie had a quakey feeling about the man Chris called "Mr. Fellner" instead of "Dad." She decided that maybe writers were all strange and that all the tales she had heard about this one must be true.

Chapter 6

The Depression was losing its grip on the South, and the Sivley family was receiving some checks from an Oklahoma oil company. Helen Sivley was now alone in the old Sivley home, and she was a lady of some means and considerable good looks. If anyone ever believed otherwise it had never been received well. Helen was almost on par with George Parkes in reputation and largesse. She owned some acreage around her big home, and the only occupant of the fenced back lot was a majestic bull. No one dared to enter the fenced back ten acres because of this almost black behemoth that ruled there. Because of his enormous size and disposition she had named him "Beware", and he lived a very special life in his barn and with special care.

One bright and early morning the man who did chores for Helen Sivley found Beware dead in his barn. There was no wound, no sign of a struggle, nothing except a small amount of white foam around his muzzle and on the ground near him. Helen was angry and grieved. For some reason she felt that this was against her personally, and she did not accept the fact that he might have just died - - no, Helen felt in her very bones that someone had killed him. It was a long time before she let the subject drop, and she bought a very large and fierce looking dog that received the special treatment in her home that Beware had received in his barn. Almost as a remembrance of Beware, she named him "Junior".

It was only three days to the day that Len, Helen's newly-hired gardener, had come to her kitchen door with the news that some strange looking people were occupying the back of the ten acres and had set up tents. Helen got in her Jeep with him and they drove to the camp. It was Gypsies, and there seemed to be about twenty of them. Helen was furious. She stormed over to the one who seemed to be in charge. He was a dark, swarthy man with colorful clothing and beaded moccasins on his feet.

In the early 1930's, Gypsies often arrived in small towns in the South and more than likely they were unwelcome. Usually when they moved away, often at night, a lot of peoples' valuables left with them. Law enforcement was dedicated but inadequate.

Helen was about to tell this man she would call the law to remove them, when a woman of at least six feet or more opened the tent flap behind them and waved her hand for Helen to join her. Helen told Len to stay close by, and she entered the tent. It was beautiful. There were bright rugs on the floor, a beautiful mosaic table and flamingo-colored large cushions around the table. The walls were covered with filmy hangings in green and soft gold colors, and there was fragrance that was almost hypnotic. The woman motioned to Helen to a large cushion, and she sat down across from her.

"I am Navura, lovely lady, and I can understand your feelings about our moving onto your property. We will move on soon, but we need a time to rest from our travels. I can tell your future if you will let me, and that will be my way of thanking you if you will allow us to stay for a short time."

Her voice was soft and low and her eyes held Helen's for a long time. Navura was dark and elegant looking, and she was wearing a wrapping around her entire body of a soft gold garment tied with a sash around her waist. She held out her hand and on the middle finger was a large ring which seemed to change colors in the glow of the two oil lamps on each side of them. Her hand was smooth and slender and graceful. Helen could not take her eyes off the shimmering beauty of the ring.

Navura began to examine Helen's outstretched hand, and she began to chant softly.

"Helen Sivley, you are a very privileged woman. You will never marry again. But you will be very happy. Your husband died over a year ago, and you have begun to be your true self again. You lost a strange but beloved pet not long ago, but you have acquired another. You have a very kind heart, and you will let us stay a few weeks. Your servant awaits you. I, Navura, am your friend. Now you may go."

Helen left without a word, and she and Len left the circle of tents with only the one man standing by the cook pot in the circle. He was seemingly unaware of their leaving.

Len looked straight ahead as he drove the Jeep back across the field. Finally, he addressed Helen. "Miz Sivley, are you O.K.?" Helen nodded. She was just beginning to feel like she could breathe again.

Len tried again. "Did she scare you, Miz Sivley?" She shook her head. He continued. "That man was cooking some stew, Miz Sivley. It was beef stew, I believe- Surely did smell good." Helen did not answer.

When they got back to her house, she went in without a word. Helen went into her room and sat before the mirror looking at her reflection. She thought about what she had just experienced, and she felt elated and more excited than she had felt in a long time.

Oakville always celebrated Halloween in the Community House, and Helen was usually the main hostess. She helped decorate the big room where the people brought food and danced, and the kids had games and won prizes. Helen supplied all the prizes for go-fishing and pin-the-tail-on-the-donkey, but she left early.

"Helen's not herself these days," Hettie told Nellie. She is never home anymore, and no one seems to know where she goes. It's not my business, but Myrtle said she had seen her at that fortune teller's booth on the edge of town several times. I can't imagine why in the world she lets them stay on her place much less visiting with them.

Nellie sighed. "These people scare me," she said. I sure don't want her tellin' my fortune."

For sure, Novura had acquired a friend. She had begun to tell Helen some of her secrets. She did not hesitate to tell Helen to get herself a large ring similar to the one she wore. She even acquired it for her with Helen's money. The occult soon had a willing and accomplished disciple.

When the Gypsies left, Helen Sivley left with them. She left her property for her lawyer to manage, and she would contact him monthly where to send her a check or money order. She took Junior with her. It was fortunate that Helen Sivley was "well-fixed".

Helen had learned well, and soon she had more customers in her tent at the stops they made all through the West than Novura did, and Novura began to resent her. She even tried to turn the rest of the clan against her, but with little success. Even Mada, the head clansman, was showing Helen too much attention.

It was three years after Helen Sivley left Oakville with the Gypsy caravan that she was found in her tent with stab wounds all over her upper body, bloody, and with her face utterly destroyed by a chemical. Mada found her. The murder was never reported. They buried her and left, moving on to another camp. Jake Smith, her lawyer, not having heard from her again, finally settled her Estate. She still had her home, but her bank account was gone.

Oakville had lost a good and well-liked citizen and there was much talk about Gypsies. The talk was not good. When Gypsies appeared in Oakville again, they were turned away. After a time it was almost that Helen Sivley had never lived except for Len. He never forgot her.

Len became a well-respected citizen of Oakville. He was a good man. He had come to Oakville with a small satchel of clothes and nothing else. He was 38 years old at the time and had walked to Oakville from Memphis, catching a ride part of the way with a trucker. He had served three years in jail for being in the wrong place at the wrong time. Those three years were a living hell for a quiet, humble man who had never hurt anyone or anything.

Soon after arriving in Oakville, he noticed the big house set back from the street with the huge yard. Len was hungry, and turned in at the long driveway. Helen Sivley had noticed how much needed to be done in her huge yard and was out raking around the side door when he walked up. He called to her before approaching her, and Helen turned to him without any sign of fear.

"Lady, I noticed you might need a little help, and I surely need a meal. Sure hope you can let me work for something to eat." Len was embarrassed but his stomach was beginning to hurt.

Helen motioned for him to come on in the garage and on into the kitchen. "It just happened I have some really good chicken I can fix for you and then you can work as long as you like. Joe didn't show up yesterday, and the place is a mess." She busied with the meal, and he enjoyed chicken, rolls, sliced tomatoes, and a big bowl of ice cream and chocolate cake He had never tasted anything better in his life.

"Thank you, Ma'am, I am ready to work if you will show me where the rake and stuff are." Helen led him to the shed in the back and left him there and went inside.

Len worked the rest of the day, and he only quit when it got dark. He saw the light on in the kitchen and went to the door. Helen was waiting for him.

"Heavenly days, man, don't you ever know when to quit? I fixed your supper." Len was thankful. That wonderful lunch had left him with an even bigger need for food. She had made him two ham sandwiches and tea and another piece of cake. Len ate quietly, and she came to the table with a glass of tea and observed him as he consumed the food.

"I didn't even ask your name, and I hope you will come back tomorrow. There is so much to do around here." Len was nonplussed over the ease she showed being around him. His thoughts were if she knew he was a jail-bird, she would be afraid of him. He really didn't know her. Helen Sivley wasn't afraid of anyone.

"My name is Len Mitchell, and I will be here early in the morning. Thank you Ma'am." He got up to leave.

"Do you have a place to stay tonight?" Helen asked. "I have a bed in the storeroom, and you can use the bathroom in the back hall if you want to stay." He nodded. She showed him the way, and he noticed she locked the door in between the main house and the storeroom. He was glad. He didn't want this wonderful woman to be careless in anyway with anyone.

Len stayed. Helen fixed up his room with some comforts, and he worked all that year for lodging and a decent salary. He earned his pay, and when Beware was found dead and he left to see about disposing of the carcass, he was angry with himself that the body of the big bull was gone when he returned. He could not believe his eyes when he got back with the back-hoe that nothing was there to bury. No one ever found any trace of it for many years, and Paul Jones said that some hungry people must have taken it for food. He hoped it wasn't poisoned meat. Something had killed that big creature. The whole case was a mystery puzzle and room for much talk in Oakville. The Gypsies were questioned with no answers.

Len Mitchell became an accepted part of Oakville life. His blond hair, blue eyes, and handsome physique became welcome in most circles, and welcomed in every home, especially those with eligible Oakville ladies. His small house was a gathering place for men that lived alone. Len Mitchell had found his place.

It was almost a year before the estate of Helen Sivley was settled. Her lawyer had to pay the taxes and see to the house and grounds because Helen Sivley didn't have a will or any close family. He hired Len to work the place and keep the yard which Len would have tried to do anyway because of his feelings for Helen.

No word from anywhere or anyone had come, so her disappearance was soon forgotten by most when seismograph people asked and paid for rights to make tests on the back ten acres. Her lawyer signed the papers and used the money to do repairs on the house. Len spent all his free time there hoping beyond hope that someone would hear from Helen.

It was like a thunderstorm hit when the chief engineer called her lawyer and told him that they had found a skeleton buried where they were working, and even more astounding, underneath the bones of a person, were the bones of a huge animal. It only took a short time of thought that Jake Smith knew what had happened to Helen's bull. His first thought was that the human skeleton was Helen, but further examination showed it had been a male. Who it was they never found out, but the findings almost made

Len sick. The Gypsies had taken Helen away, and he was unsure that she had left of her own accord. These people were thieves and even murderers, and he never had a day that he didn't think of the woman he loved and he never gave up hope, but Len waited in vain. Helen Sivley's grave was never found but her story was told all over the country.

Mada was caught burying a body in Arizona, and was incoherent when he was taken to jail. Navura had used a hatchet on another woman, and had sent Mada out to get rid of the body. Mada had consumed a whole bottle of whiskey, and he chose a place not far from the highway. A Highway Patrolman saw his truck and investigated. The Gypsy angle to the story brought a lot of attention, and Len saw the headlines. It confirmed what he had always believed. His hope was gone, but his love for Helen lasted all his life.

One thing for sure, Len Mitchell knew when he smelled beef stew cooking in the Gypsy pot that night and he also knew what happened to Beware. His only regret was that he didn't know for sure what happened to Helen.

Chapter 7

Miss Maggie lived down the street from the Walkers, and she and Sissie became friends. Whenever Sissie was feeling especially lonely, she would walk down Elm Street, and each house she passed she observed closely for a sign of someone that she could visit with for just a moment. Sissie was lonely, a lot, and she often wondered if anyone in the houses she passed needed company. She always ended up at Miss Maggie's. Maggie Rutherford's father had been the editor of the <u>Oakville News</u>, and for a small town paper it was a good newspaper. When Tom Rutherford died, his only child, Margaret, took over and was successful for thirty-nine years. She never married. When she sold the paper, she retired to her home on Elm Street with her two dogs as her companions.

As time went by, she took in every dog and cat that needed a home, and mostly stayed in the back three rooms of her house. Her backyard was fenced with wide, closely-boarded wood, eight feet high. The neighborhood kids often tried to peek through, but there was not an open space in that wall. Miss Maggie didn't want anyone to see how much her family "had grown." When anyone came to see her, they were cordially invited to the front parlor and no where else. Even Sissie, her favorite visitor, never left the front parlor but the sounds in the back were very close by and very evident.

Sissie liked to visit Miss Maggie, and they would sit in the parlor and talk like two school teachers. Miss Maggie was amazed at the young girl's grasp of life and the world in general. She usually had a small gift to give Sissie each time she came. One time it would be a tiny vase or a small figurine - - once even she served her cookies and lemonade in small, delicate china and crystal with linen napkins and fine linen on the table she brought in from the kitchen. Sissie never doubted that it was clean, it was so elegant. Sissie never stayed too long, and the two of them became best of friends.

Few in Oakville knew how old Miss Maggie was and no one dared ask anymore than to ask her how many dogs and cats she had. The place didn't smell bad so her secrets were acceptable seeing that it was who she was - - Miss Maggie Rutherford.

The morning she died was the morning that Sissie had decided to visit earlier than usual, as she had made a cake and wanted to take some to Miss Maggie. She knocked and knocked, and the dogs were howling so loud that Sissie decided she should call her Dad and see if someone would check on her. She ran home and called him. Dr. Walker left his office and drove to Miss Maggie's house. Sure enough, something seemed wrong so he went to his house and called Paul Jones. Paul joined him back at the Rutherford's house and finally found a way in. Sure enough, Miss Maggie was dead in her bed probably having been there for a couple of days.

They could not believe their eyes when they entered the back part of the house. One room had thirty some-odd cats all hungry and needing water and fourteen dogs all hungry and barking. It took several days for the animals to be taken and put in cages down on the Square. Many of them were adopted but many of them were put to sleep. It took even more time to have the house cleaned and fumigated.

Sissie was devastated. She had a very strong attachment to this lady and she cried herself to sleep a many a night. She cried not only for herself but for the many pets that had to be destroyed. Dr. Walker let her have one small black and white dog that no one else wanted. Sissie loved and cared for little Miss Maggie for many years never forgetting or completely letting go of her good friend who had listened and needed her too.

Chapter 8

Myrtle Barnes was Hettie's best friend, and they looked forward to hearing from each other each day. If one day was missed, both of them could hardly wait to hear from the other. Myrtle didn't have a phone, so she would get in her little Chevy and drive into Oakville early enough to have a cup of coffee, maybe a doughnut or coffee cake that Hettie always had ready. She couldn't stay long because Caswell, her husband, didn't want Myrtle out of his sight and she always hurried home after her visits in Oakville.

Myrtle was forty-eight years old, but looked ten years older, but little means to do anything about it. Caswell liked it that way. Never, or almost never, did she complain about her marriage. She had grown up on a farm with parents that lived extremely well for farm people. Her father worked seven hundred acres that he had inherited, and he was probably the most successful farmer anywhere in that county. Myrtle had grown up with most anything she wanted within reason. Being an only child, she was always on the go, rode a beautiful gelding and dated several popular boys in high school.

When Myrtle married Caswell Ponder, everyone who had known her were surprised. Caswell was about as ordinary looking as any man could be. He was average in height, weight and personality. In addition, he had three big warts on his face and neck. He finished the sixth grade and began farming his small farm when he was less than twenty. His family had left him a four room house with no phone, no refinements, and no indoor plumbing. Myrtle loved Caswell and she went about her life with no excitement but a semblance of happiness. They had their first child after fourteen months and they named her Ruby. Ruby was to follow in Momma's footsteps. She married an alcoholic with no special qualities except meanness.

Myrtle's second child was named Lillian. Lillian was born fat and stayed fat all her life. Lillian married a man who had been gassed in World War I, and they lived on his monthly check from the government.

Myrtle was often going to ask Hettie to come out, but never got around to it. They visited at Hettie's and it suited them both.

When Myrtle didn't show up one day, Hettie got worried and finally on the third day of Myrtle not showing up she drove out to Myrtle's house. Caswell was sick and Myrtle was beside herself. He would not let her call the doctor, as he said he would be okay. Besides they could not afford a doctor to drive out there to see him. Hettie stayed and cooked a good meal with the garden vegetables she found in the ice box. She had only been there once before and she had to ask Myrtle where the bathroom was. For the first time since they had become close friends, she hesitated and looked embarrassed. It was to the left in the backyard. Hettie found the little building and when she opened the door she drew back. The odor was terrible. It was what people called a "two holer" and the toilet paper was a Sears and Roebuck catalog. Hettie got out of there as fast as she could and returned to the house with a new respect for Myrtle. How in heavens name, thought Hettie, could Myrtle live like this when she had come from such better circumstances. She never once complained and Hettie now understood why she was never asked out there.

The visits between the two became non-existent after that day, and Hettie missed her friend so much. She received a note after three weeks that Caswell was much worse. And, Myrtle had to call a doctor. Caswell refused to go to the hospital, and Myrtle could not leave him even for an hour. Caswell died the day she wrote the letter, and Hettie drove out uninvited. Myrtle buried Caswell in the little cemetery down the road at the little church she attended. That was his first time in the church. There were about thirty people at the services and several vases of home grown flowers. Myrtle did not cry nor did the two girls. This man's death could only be described as his life - - - ordinary.

Chapter 9

The South had settled into the Depression as everyone was calling the scarcity of money. The banks were failing all over the Nation, and only one out of the three in Oakville was still open. Latham Parkes was 68 years old and a lion of a man. He stood six feet six inches tall and carried his 280 pounds with dignity and pride. He still made every call on the bank good, and he had the respect and a little fear of everyone in his town. He drove a black Packard that stood in the same parking spot every day for thirty some-odd years. He kept many a small business from closing its doors, and he would drive down Elm Street at exactly 8:45 every morning to the bank. He opened the doors himself.

Latham Parkes had only one soft spot left in his heart, and that was his grandson, Latham Parkes, Jr. The grandfather called his namesake "Tad". He never told anyone why, but Tad knew why—his Grandfather had referred to him as "Tadpole" until he was starting to school –but only when the two of them were alone. It was their secret. When Latham's older son, John, was offered an engineering job in Oklahoma, and took it, it almost broke the old man's heart. Betty Jean, Latham's wife of 48 years, had died of cancer and losing Tad too had left Latham lonely and unable to socialize in anyway. His big house at the end of Elm Street remained quiet and dark for nearly five years when his sister, Hettie, invited herself for a visit and never left. Hettie had no place to go, so it was settled. She took the back bedroom upstairs, and it wasn't long before she made things better in Latham's big house. She was a good cook, and she prepared luscious meals which Latham grudgingly complimented and quietly consumed.

It was the year 1939, and Tad was coming to see his Grandfather all by himself. He was 19 years old and had grown up in luxury. John had more than succeeded in his Oklahoma move. And Latham was proud of his son and had forgiven him for leaving him. For the first time in years Latham was excited - - he was to have Tad all to himself. Latham even had the house painted, and he asked the housekeeper to fix up Tad's room upstairs.

Tad was handsome. He entered his grandfather's house with open arms, and his grandfather, great aunt and Betty, the housekeeper, were completely captivated. He had only been in Oakville for two days when Ned Mitchell called him and asked him to double-date the next evening. Tad and Ned had played together as kids, and Tad said he'd be ready anytime. Ned had a date with Nell Green and he would get Tad a good-looking date. Tad had no trouble getting the big black Packard for the evening. Ned thought about the available girls, and decided to call the one he would really like to date himself - - Sissie Walker.

Sissie was almost startled when Ned called, as Ned was 20 years old, and she had never been out with his crowd. He explained about Tad, and she agreed to go. The four of them drove straight to Sargeance's Bluff to a dance hall of good reputation and a good dance floor. All the college kids drove there to dance and meet friends. No alcohol was served, and the nickelodeon had all the good records—one being "Apple Blossom Time". Tad fell in love that night dancing with the prettiest girl he had ever seen. "Apple Blossom Time" rang in his ears for the rest of his life, and Ned had to ask him to choose another tune. They drank cokes and danced until nearly twelve, when Sissie told them she needed to get home.

Tad took Nell and Ned home first, and when they got to the front door at Sissie's, he caught her shoulders and kissed her soundly on the mouth. He left with neither of them saying a word. At ten the next morning, he was calling; and they planned to go to the Bluff that evening alone. "Apple Blossom Time" rang in his ears all day, and he pulled up in front of her house a little puzzled by the way this girl had affected him. They had no trouble talking as he drove, and when they arrived they had a cold drink and a sandwich and they danced. The time passed so fast, it was almost midnight when she told him she needed to go home. Her Dad was pretty lenient with her, as he knew she was out with Latham's grandson. When they arrived at the house, Tad drew her down to the old rattan settee on the big front porch, and he kissed her. He held her and they sat there together completely mesmerized with each other. As Sissie remembered through the years, they smooched - - that's all she could call it. She had to break away from him and tell him she had to go in. Tad was supposed to return to Oklahoma the next day, but he did not. He stayed another day and night, and his father called and told him that college was waiting and to catch the next train home. Oklahoma was a long way from Mississippi, but Tad was to never forget his first love, nor did Sissie. Latham Parkes was to move to Oklahoma later, leaving his bank and his big house to his two nephews who lived in St. Louis, Missouri.

George and David Parkes moved south and joined Aunt Hettie in the big house on Elm Street.

Oakville had its beautiful women, and Latham's wife, Betty Jean, was one of them. More than that, she was tall and fascinating to watch as she walked into any room anywhere. Her looks affected everyone, but she was almost a social recluse. She did not participate in many of the social affairs in Oakville, as she told her husband, Latham, that she did not really enjoy small talk or party food. So, few people knew Betty Jean Parkes well. She did attend church on Sunday morning, and she saw that her two sons were there for Sunday School. She liked people, but she liked them from a distance. Whatever she liked Latham honored. He adored her and often sat and watched her every move as they went about their quiet lives in Oakville.

Their two sons, John and James, were good athletes and participated in every sport the school offered. James quarterbacked the Oakville football team, and John played baseball and ran track. All in all, the Parkes family lived an "All American" family life, and Betty Jean was happy in her home and her garden. Her roses were evident in the church many Sundays and in the hospital rooms at the only hospital in town. Betty Jean did visit in the hospital regularly and soon became well known to the staff there. Her best friend was the Registered Nurse, Jo Ann Gibson, and they had lunch together when Jo Ann could get away. Since she was the only graduate nurse in the hospital, it was often difficult for her to have time enough to eat lunch.

Jo Ann was not good looking, but she was very much in evidence wherever she went. She was self-confident, smart, and a fine professional. She took an instant liking to Betty Jean, and they soon became close friends. Betty Jean spent time with the patients until Jo Ann could get free, and often Jo Ann brought lunch for the two of them and they would sit in the small Lounge and eat and talk. Betty Jean liked nothing better, and Jo Ann was the one good friend she needed.

Later, when Betty Jean really needed her, Jo Ann was there for her.

Betty Jean would visit the patient rooms and leave small vases of roses wherever she went. It was there she met Lavinia Thorp, a 57 year old woman who had terminal cancer. Betty Jean would sit and read to Lavinia, sometimes from the Bible and sometimes from the newspaper. Lavinia was also losing her sight and now could only see shadows. Betty Jean tried to visit her regularly, and Lavinia began to confide in her. Lavinia had an only son, married to a harried, bullied woman who was afraid of him to the extent that she obeyed his every word and remembered his every threat. He hated his mother.

Lavinia owned a home and a car and lovely antique furnishings which he began selling without her knowledge. He had put her in the hospital only after much urging by her friends. He said his mother was going to die anyway, so she might as well stay at home and die. He would send his wife to see her once a week, mostly in hopes that she had passed on.

Betty Jean decided to confront him one day after leaving Lavinia's hospital room with Lavinia in tears and so pitiful that Betty Jean could hardly stand it. He was going to send his mother to The Poor House, which was supported by the County. Lavinia was not a poor woman, but her son had confiscated most of her belongings.

Betty Jean did not tell Latham or Jo Ann where she was going, but she drove out to the son's home, and with all the dignity she could conjure up, she knocked on the door. Reese Thorp came to the door with almost a snarl on his face and rudely asked her what she wanted. She told him in no uncertain terms that Lavinia was very ill and could not be moved. He moved forward pushing the door and Lavinia fell backwards off the porch onto the pile of bricks next to the steps. He called his wife, and she called the police. He claimed she fell before he even opened the door. Betty never recovered from her fall. She had the best of care and all the love a wife could have, but she only lived three weeks. She was never able to tell anyone exactly what happened.

Latham Parkes retired into a shell. He never married again. Most of his heart died with her. He had no alternative but to accept Reese Thorp's version of the accident, but Reese Thorp never dared to face Latham again for the rest of his life. Day and night, Latham Parkes was his adversary. Thorp could not have picked two worse characters to invade his nighttime. His night dreams became so bad that he had to be taken to the hospital where Jo Ann presided.

One good thing came out of the whole bad mess. Thorp's wife got Lavinia out of the hospital, and she cared for her in Lavinia's lovely home until Lavinia died. Thorp died in the night at the hospital. It was said that he had a terrible nightmare and that he died of fright. Jo Ann signed the Death Certificate.

Chapter 10

George Parkes was a duplicate of his Uncle Latham, tall, big and silent. He had graduated from Yale with honors, and knew exactly how to run a business. David was the more outgoing of the two, but had been partially paralyzed in a car accident and was in a wheelchair. He had graduated from the University of Missouri and was the Accountant of the two. They took over the bank and the bank thrived. Somehow, they worked in harmony - - George as bank President but David carrying most of the load. They learned to love Aunt Hettie and she loved them. The Parkes house lit up inside and out,

George needed a fill-in secretary for the summer. Latham's efficient lady had surgery, and George asked Ned Mitchell if he knew of someone. Ned knew that Sissie had honors in high school business classes, and he recommended her for the job. George hired her. He called her Sarah , and he appreciated her in every way. Sarah would be seventeen in the fall, and she was a beautiful girl. She knew that Mr. George Parkes was interested in more than her typing and shorthand, but she never showed her feelings in the bank. Finally, one rainy afternoon as she was leaving, he asked her if he could take her home and maybe stop by The Manse and have a bite to eat. They talked easily, and before many more days, they were the talk of Oakville. "Why George Parkes is old enough to be her father" was said on every corner.

George, usually so silent and almost stoic, opened up his heart to Sarah, and she responded. The first time he kissed her, he knew he would ask her to marry him the day she turned eighteen. Dr. Walker seemed agreeable, and on the day after her 18th birthday, George asked her to marry him. Sarah was now her official name, as few denied George his preferences. They dined together through that year, rode through the countryside in his big car, and attended church together every Sunday. Sarah felt a deep affection for this dignified man who desired her complete attention. They were married in a small wedding, and she went to the big house after their trip to New York. George defied anyone to discuss their ages, and soon the talk stopped and their relationship was accepted. They saw several shows there, and George consummated their marriage to his satisfaction, but leaving his young bride with a lot of questions about the marriage bed. Sarah had no regrets even then, but she did look at her fine looking husband with a different feeling. It was with more respect than passion, and accepted his gifts of candy and flowers with warmth and frequent embraces. George loved Sarah and was proud of her. He intended for Oakville to welcome her as its new social leader. Being Mrs. George Parkes, that was assured.

Sarah began to use her energies in changing many things in their home. She bought new curtains for their bedroom and new drapes and lamps for the living room. Even George Parkes went slowly with monetary matters, and he called her into the den one evening and asked her to slow down a bit, but he smiled at her as he said it and kissed her on the forehead. Money still was not too plentiful all over the Nation. Sarah turned to playing bridge and joining Hettie in the kitchen.

The Depression was lifting and people began to shop a little more. One of the two theaters opened again and started selling popcorn again and both were crowded on Saturdays. One of the other banks re-opened and more cars surrounded the Courthouse on weekdays. On Saturdays, the big watermelons were bringing as much as a quarter, and Mr. Eades was selling his fresh vegetables as fast as he could load his buggy and deliver them. Mr. Eades used his buggy and never even considered exchanging Molly, his red mare, for a car. Mr. Eades was on the street all that summer with his wares and only pre-deceased Molly by six months. No one ever knew which one was older, Molly by horse years, or Mr. Eades by human. His daughter always maintained that Molly died of grief.

Chapter 11

The first year of marriage passed rapidly for Sarah, as she had a lot to learn not only about her husband but the big house and how he wanted it run. George had changed some in those twelve months, and Sarah found herself more and more alone. George had begun to work later and was more silent than before, and she blamed herself. She finally, after another several months of spending most of her evenings without him, she found herself turning to Hettie for companionship. She and David played gin, and he often stayed down the hall with her and Hettie and talked about the day at the bank. David could almost feel the bewilderment this beautiful girl felt as more and more George was gone. George bought a small farm west of town and began to drive there after banking hours. David finally said something to him about his absences and reminded him he had a young wife who needed him. George began to set times for Sarah to meet him downtown for dinner, and he even took her to a movie some weekends; but he seemed to be shielding himself from any intimacy with his young wife. Sarah found a puppy on the street north of the Courthouse one cold winter day, and she picked the

Melanie Maniver

shivering little creature up, put her in her car and took her home.
She decided the minute those big brown eyes met hers that George
could say what he liked, but the dog would stay. She named
her "Mariah" and like the wind she was forever moving, silently
touching and warm. It was a beautiful answer to a problem, and
David often smiled as he watched them together. Mariah sat in
the chair with Sarah as she read or knitted, slept by her bed, which
Sarah now occupied alone, and sat close always if Sarah was busy.
She ran like the wind outside, and fetched whatever Sarah threw
for her. She even began to fetch Sarah's bedroom shoes for her at
night and put them by the bed. Hettie talked to Mariah in much
the same way Sarah did—as though the dog were another person.
David caught himself doing the same thing at times. George knew
Mariah was there, but he gave her no attention. Mariah returned
the favor. She grew to about 65 pounds and was known all over
the neighborhood by name and by reputation. She never left her
yard and no one entered it without her permission. She knew
the neighbors and they all knew her and appreciated having her
around. Mariah had found her place, and Sarah loved her dearly.

Sarah often sat by the window facing north in a big old padded
rocker, and Mariah sat by her side, no longer finding enough
room in the chair. Sarah watched the old cedar tree in the yard
as it yielded to the wind only slightly and she often cried quietly.
Mariah would lay her head on Sarah's knees and try to comfort
her as best she could. Sarah had finally confronted her husband,
asking him if he still wanted her as his wife and she forced herself
to tell him she was lonely and she wanted to bear him a child. He
looked away and did not respond for a long time.

"Sarah, I have given you most everything anyone could want.
You can go anywhere, do anything, have most anything you want.
A child is not in the picture for me. You knew when you married

48

me that I am considerably older than you, and children get on my nerves. As far as I am concerned, you can find another way to be happy. I do love you and I am proud of the fact that you are my wife, that should be enough, and I think it would be with most any other woman.´ With that, he got up, put down the paper he was reading and went to his room.

Sarah sat there for a long time, the darkness outside so dense she felt it enter her very soul. She sat in the dark until David wheeled past the door. Not wanting him to see her swollen face from crying, she slipped out the other door and went outside. She sat for a long time in the old swing in the side yard, wondering how in the world she had failed so badly in her marriage that her husband did not want her much less a child. She didn't want to tell her troubles to Hettie, but there was no one else. Her friends all told her how lucky she was to be married to such a handsome guy who was so good to her. "George spoils you something awful," she heard many times, and she always agreed. Loyalty was one quality that Sarah believed in, and she would never belittle her husband to anyone.

Chapter 12

*I*t was midnight when she finally went to her room, and the only light on in the house was in David's room. For the first time since she had come to live in this big house, she wanted to knock on his door and be welcomed in, as she knew she would be. David was so unlike his older brother, and she felt easy around him. Often when they played gin or he was trying to teach her to play chess, they laughed and joked about her inability to master the art of chess. David had often asked her how in the world she won prizes in bridge when she was so dense at the chess board. She would ask him why in the world he never, or almost never, won at gin. They were good friends. She resisted the temptation to knock and went on to her room. She sat at her dresser after putting on the beautiful gown and negligee George had brought her from New York. The business he had invested in there was evidently doing well, but he never discussed it with her. She looked at herself in the oval mirror and smoothed her hair back from her face. She was a little heavier than on her wedding day, and Aunt Hettie echoed her friends, that it was becoming. Why does George not want me, she asked herself? Her answer was always the same - - I don't know. She didn't sleep well that night at all. Mariah joined her in the big bed, and they watched the moon outside the window together for a very long time. The moon was just a sliver –like her thoughts.

The next evening all four were home, and they went to the den where there was a group of comfortable chairs. George was reading, Hettie was knitting and David was napping in his chair. Sarah felt happy and comforted for the first time in a long while. Mariah was close by. This is my family, she thought. Dad is gone, and I can hardly remember my Mother. My sister is in Ohio with her family, and here I am in the house at the end of the street in the town I grew up in, married to the richest and handsomest man anywhere around. I should be happy all the time. I guess being in the same room with Mariah at my feet and all of us together makes me ashamed of all the tears I have shed. She laid her magazine aside when she noticed that George had fallen asleep in his chair. In the seven years they had been married she had never seen him so relaxed. She studied the man whose name she carried, and she realized that she really did not know him. He would be embarrassed if he snored or his posture was not just right. George had to be in control of himself and his surroundings at all times, and he could not be any other way. She realized that she would either have to accept that or ask him for a divorce. She studied his face as he slept, and she knew she would never leave him. She would try to be happy and to be the wife he wanted her to be - - attractive, always there and dignified. She felt older than her years, and she knew that would please him. He has beautiful hands, she thought. I always look at a man's hands for some reason. She smiled at Hettie and she and Mariah left the room. She knew that George would wake wondering if he had embarrassed himself by falling asleep in his chair in her presence. I guess I understand him better than I realize, and I like the way he is she thought almost aloud to Mariah.

Chapter 13

Sarah slept late the next day, and she had to hurry to get to the mid service. She did not go home for lunch but joined Nancy Tomas after church. They went to the new restaurant in town, and they were hardly seated before Nancy caught her hand and tears clouded her eyes.

"Sarah, I just have to talk to somebody, and I know you won't repeat this; but I think Sam is seeing someone else. The kids never see him anymore, and when I see him he is hurrying around trying to leave the house. I fix good meals and I try to look nice for him but he doesn't notice anymore. I might as well be the door frame in the bedroom these days. You and George seem to have such a wonderful relationship. I don't know what to do." She stopped and looked at her friend, embarrassed but eager to be heard. Sarah was folding her napkin back and forth and forced herself to look into Nancy's eyes. She wanted to say the right words, but her response was muted because of her own situation at home. She so wanted to sympathize, but she knew from experience that encouragement meant more than sympathy. She held on to Nancy's hand and patted it as she thought of her answer.

"Nancy, don't give up on your marriage. I've learned a lot these last seven years, and it's best to hang on. You have two wonderful children, and they need their Dad. Sam may have problems other than another woman, and you need to be there for him. As for me, I would give anything to have one child, but George and I haven't been as blessed as you. Give Sam a chance to straighten out whatever is bothering him - - it may not be what you think."

Nancy smiled wanly and the waitress came to take their order. They both ordered shrimp, a salad and fried green tomatoes and both ate heartily.

"Just talking has helped a lot, Sarah. Thanks. And wasn't that good shrimp?" They paid their individual checks and left the café, Nancy to pick up her two boys at her Mother's and Sarah to go home to be there when Hettie returned. She planned to fix something light and good for supper and hoped David would join them, which he did.

George arrived home that night earlier than expected, and he surprised Sarah with a beautifully wrapped package. She sat on the couch in the den and opened the box with eager anticipation. He had brought her gifts from many of his other trips to New York, but she was overwhelmed when she saw the beautiful necklace and earrings. She wore the large diamond he had given her when they married with pride, and now she asked him to fasten the necklace for her as she put the earrings on. As he clasped it, she turned and put her arms around him. He held her close only a moment and went into his office without a word.

That night the rain came down in torrents and lightning flashed across her room as great crashes of thunder sounded. Mariah crouched down beside her on the big bed, and Sarah pulled the cover over her. She wanted to go into George's room and crawl in bed with him, but she couldn't make herself do it. She and Mariah slept fitfully until long past midnight the storm stopped. Mariah woke her the next morning jumping down from the bed, signaling a need to go out. The house was still quiet, so she put her robe and slippers on and went to the kitchen. As she let Mariah out the back door, she heard David's wheelchair coming down the hall. The coffee was already made, and the aroma was overwhelming.

"Coffee smells better than it tastes, doesn't it? David smiled and pulled up to the breakfast table. She poured two cups and got the sugar bowl. David looked at her with a deep affection. "Sarah, you are some kind of a woman. You put up with my brother's seeming indifference. He loves you, you know." David sipped his coffee. He never looked away but looked into her eyes with a look that made her a little afraid. He would not let her look away, but they sat there silently for a minute which seemed much longer to Sarah.

"If you ever get tired of his strange ways, and you want to make a change, let me know. I happen to love you very much, and it's partly George's fault that I have let it happen to me. He's gone half the time, leaving us here together, and, Sarah," he reached and caught her hand, "you are the most desirable woman I have ever met. I may be in a wheelchair but I am every bit a man, so don't sell me short. I told my big, quiet, efficient brother the same thing I am telling you, so don't feel that I am going behind his back. He knows how I feel and now you do too." David let her hand go, but he continued to keep his eyes riveted on her face. They sipped their coffee, and Sarah watched as he finished his coffee and put his cup in the sink with hers.

"Thank you, David." She left him there by the sink, rinsing his cup. She had never felt so shaky in her whole life. She walked slowly to her room and then walked to the adjoining bedroom, George's room. There was not one article out of place. She never felt free to go in but now she walked slowly into the big room where her husband slept alone.

"Goodness," she thought, "he's only 52 years old, and I'm still a young woman—or so Hettie tells me. I want a family so bad, and it seems that already I have waited too long." She walked into his bathroom and noticed her picture on the shelf close to the door. She smelled his shaving lotion, and she thought of the last time he had held her close and how wonderful it had felt. "I do love him so much - - crazy me!" She turned and left the room, going down the hall to the kitchen. She knew she would spend the evening with David, and she began to make a cake, mostly to keep busy. She wanted to talk to Hettie, but how in heaven could she tell anyone that she loved two brothers. Even Hettie might not understand.

Chapter 14

*I*t was past one o'clock when Sarah heard the phone, and she grabbed her robe as she ran down the hall to answer it. It was Nancy, and she was hysterical.

"Sarah, c-come here and help me. Right now, Sarah. I don't know what to do." With that, the phone clicked. Sarah ran back to her room and hurriedly dressed. David had come to his door, and she yelled back at him that she was going to the Tomases'. She drove quickly to the next street and pulled up in front of an almost dark house. She ran to the front door, found it unlocked and went in. She heard Nancy crying in the back, and she carefully followed the light to the back.

"Oh, Sarah, Sam has locked himself in the bathroom and won't answer me. I've pleaded with him, but I'm so afraid. I hate to wake the kids, but I just know he's doing something terrible to himself. I've tried everything. I don't know what to do, Sarah. Tell me, Sarah."

Sarah listened with her head against the door. She tried the door, but it was securely locked. "Sam" she called, "You're scaring Nancy to death. Please come out and talk to her. You don't want her to wake the kids and cause all kinds of trouble. Open the door." She stood back. But there was no response,

"Nancy, you'll have to call the police. Someone needs to see what he is doing or what he has done. Can I call them for you? You go on in with your children and prepare them for whatever we find.' Sarah went to the phone, and it was not but a few minutes before the police car drove up, and Wally Jones came in, he called to Sam through the door. There was no answer. He threw his shoulder against the door, and it opened with a crash. On the floor, in a puddle of blood, lay Sam Tomas. He had cut both wrists and was dead. Wally Jones was a seasoned policeman, but even he turned away. Sam Tomas was a friendly respected citizen, and Wally was almost as shocked as Sarah. They closed the door to the bedroom, and Wally told the women to go in the kitchen. Nancy had rejoined Sarah in the hall, and Sarah put her arm around Nancy and led her into the kitchen. She made some coffee while Wally called the Coroner and an ambulance. The two children had gotten up and were so bewildered they hardly said anything. Nancy and the children dressed and went home with Sarah. They were there for another day. The funeral was one of the largest Oakville had ever seen. Not even Nancy knew at the time why Sam would do such a thing. Later, David discussed the details with Sarah that Sam had mishandled a considerable amount of money.

"Do you mean STOLE a lot of money, David? It's hard to believe that." Sarah looked at David in disbelief. David did not elaborate, but told her some of it had been recovered. Nancy had left town with her two children who needed to be left some semblance of pride in their father. They would grow up in the west with their Mother, and they never returned to Oakville. She and Sarah had a lifelong friendship on the phone and by letter, and Sarah was thankful that Nancy did marry again to a kind and wonderful man. Sarah made two trips to see her and found her happy—and as Nancy said "pleasingly plump." Nancy was the one complete confidante that Sarah had, and she never encouraged Sarah to leave George. She maintained "he is wonderful."

Chapter 15

Winter was in the air, and she and Mariah began to take long walks in the woods behind the house. The air was crisp and invigorating and Mariah barked and ran here and there as leaves fell and crunched under their feet. There was a trail through the woods, and she and Mariah followed it to the big overhang where the neighborhood kids got together in the summer. There was a large area of sand, clean and golden, below the overhang; and she almost wanted to go below, pile up the sand, and jump into it from above as they did in her childhood. There were Phyllis, Jimmy, Jack and Louise taking turns jumping, and she always had tried to jump the fartherest. They had always brought something to eat, and sandy and dirty as they were, they would spread their food and eat at the top of the hill. She was never afraid in the woods with Mariah. It was good to remember and to relish some happy memories.

When they returned to the house, David was sitting on the spacious, screened back porch. It was Saturday and George was in New York to return on Monday. Her cheeks were flushed and her hair windblown, and she looked particularly beautiful. He told her so. She sat down across from him, and they talked for a long time. David asked her to fix them a sandwich and a drink and to have their meal there on the porch. Hettie had gone to her friend's birthday party in Center City and would not be back until late that day.

Sarah went to the kitchen and made two big ham sandwiches, found some chips, and poured two glasses of ice tea. She always had a pitcher of tea in the refrigerator, and they enjoyed it year round. She had made an apple pie the day before, and she cut two large pieces and took the tray to the porch. They ate and talked, and Mariah got a bite of food from each of them. She gazed at Sarah with her big brown eyes pleading for another bite. It was so good to talk freely with David, she thought. He is so unlike his brother, and yet they look a good bit alike. His hands are strong and his nails are manicured. She liked his easy manner, and she often forgot the fact that he was in a wheelchair, and he seemed to forget it sometimes. He was confident and strong and attractive, and she enjoyed the evening with him. It was late when they retired to their rooms.

Chapter 16

Hettie finished her grocery shopping and drove around the square. It was a hot, sultry day like so many in sleepy southern towns, and she let the breeze, hot as it was, blow in from all four windows of her car. She thought of her friends with children, especially Sallie Burton. Sallie's son's wife was the best thing Sallie could talk about, and they had four beautiful children. Hettie loved them almost as much as Sallie did. It would be great to have a son like Mark, she thought. I've missed out on a lot, but I have a lot to be thankful for too. I have George and David and my beautiful Sarah.. She drove to the small park and parked under one of the big oak trees. No one was in the park at that hour, and she decided the groceries would be O.K. for a few minutes. Hettie thought about her life at home, and she considered what her life really meant to anyone. She had heard a good sermon the past Sunday about leaving a legacy behind when your turn comes, and she thought of what she really meant to anyone.

"I guess I'm getting old," she said aloud. "I never stopped to think about it much before, really, but Dr. Biggs got me to wondering if my life has meant anything to anybody. I think they love me, especially Sarah, and I do for them all the time. We don't have any children in the family, and I do so wish George and Sarah could have at least one. Oh, well, I guess that's out of the question. They've had a while to think about it, but I guess something is wrong somewhere. Here I sit talking to myself." She started the car, as the heat was oppressive, and a fly began buzzing around her head. She drove slowly home thinking and talking to herself. "I sometimes worry about David and Sarah being alone so much together. It's kinda like George wants it that way. Anyhow, I better get home and get dinner started. I'm hungry, and I know the others are. Even George is home tonight. He hasn't been feeling so good, and he's lost some weight. Maybe fried chicken and rice and gravy will taste good to him. I wonder if I dare try to talk to him. I guess not. He won't let me." She turned in the driveway and sure enough George's big car was in the garage.

Dinner was as perfect as Hettie could remember. She added some crowder peas and hot cornbread muffins and apple salad to the menu. Her great achievement, cocoanut cream pie, was served with coffee. George told her it was the best meal he had eaten in a long time, and she felt blessed.

Sarah helped Hettie clean up the kitchen, and they chatted as they worked. Hettie had to stir up her courage, because like all the Parkes, she was hesitant to talk on a personal basis with anyone; but she felt compelled to ask Sarah if she had noticed that George did not look his usual self.

" I think he has lost a little weight, Sarah, but he says to David that he needs to, so I have not been too concerned. I think he and David talk, but David does not tell me anything personal. I wish he would, but maybe George tells him not to—I don't know." Sarah was looking out the back window, so absorbed in her own thoughts that she dried the glass she was holding over and over, finally putting it back in the soapy water in the sink.

"Hettie, what can I do? I don't know how to break the silence that George imposes on this house - - especially with me. It's like he owns me but doesn't want to admit it. I don't know why I still love him, but I do. He's so good to me in ways that matter to a lot of women, but he's not - - "and she paused trying not to demean her husband in any way - - "he's not loving. Is there any way I can reach him? I am shy around my own husband because he demands it of me. Does that make sense?"

Hettie regarded Sarah with affectionate appreciation. This young woman was desperately trying to make a marriage work that was not at all what it should be. Hettie knew how much Sarah wanted a family, and she often wondered why in the world Sarah did not just face George squarely and ask him why won't you sleep with me? As Hettie considered this, she would see George's face looming up in her memory when he was backed in a corner, and she withdrew her question. Honestly, she thought, I'm braver than Sarah and I'd hesitate to demand anything of him. He can do more with a look and silence than most of us can do with a big stick. Anyway, how can you defy someone you love - - you can't. I guess Sarah and I *are both cowards—and she does have her pride.*

Chapter 17

 $\mathscr{S}$ heriffing around Oakville wasn't too big a task, but Wally Jones was always available for most anything. The jail was above the Sheriff's office and was one of the few brick buildings in the business area of Oakville. Wally's morning had been consumed by a misunderstanding on the Square between two farmers whose wagons got crossed up, and Jerry Plummett's melons fell out and busted. It finally got settled when it was all cleaned up and Sam Mitchell decided to replace half of them with some of his big load. That meant that Plummett wouldn't have to go home with nothing that day.

Sometimes the farmers only sold three to six melons after a whole day's wait, but that would usually be enough to buy the few necessities they needed to take home. Plummett's wife had given him a short list, and he didn't ant to show up without at least the thread and the yard of material she needed. Mitchell's melons were really nice, so they shook hands.

"Sheriff Jones," and Wally turned to the little boy he had seen earlier. "I'm Jimmy Pender, and your man at the jail hollered at me for you to come there real quick. I'm tellin' you." With that the little boy ran on down the street.

Wally turned back toward the jail wondering what in the world Luke could want that bad. Luke was at the back window peering across to the back of the stores across the street.

"Whatcha want, Luke?" Wally asked.

"That dern lil sneakin' varmint, Jess Denner, just snuck around the store over there, and three little gals are with him. You know what he's up to, that dern little rat.

He's got a nickel or dime he stole from his daughter, and he's gonna do somethin' to one of those little gals he's got back there. Better hurry - - that dern little whiskered varmint."

Wally turned and almost ran across the jail yard and into the opening behind the store across the way. Sure enough, Denner was just about to convince one of the girls to remove her little cotton britches. She had already taken the dime he had offered her, and when she saw Sheriff Jones she threw it on the ground, pulled up her britches and the three little girls took off across the way and onto the Square.

Wally grabbed Denner without a word and took him straight to the jail. Luke collared him and threw the old man in a cell.

"You dern stinkin' varmint - - when you gonna stop bothering little girls. I guess your folk'll come after you as usual, but til' then you can stink up that cell, you ratty lil varmint."

Denner said nothing. He stroked his white, trim, goatee and made himself at home. His daughter would come and get him before night. Denner settled his small, skinney frame on the cot and was soon fast asleep.

Chapter 18

*S*arah heard Hettie talking to George in his study, and she could not help but stop in the hall and listen. I hope David doesn't catch me out here eavesdropping, she thought. It seemed to be about a little girl named "Gillie", and Sarah moved closer as she heard Hettie say "George," I've never really asked you to do something for me that is as important as this, and I'm asking you now. This child has to be taken out of that house, and it has to be soon. You can do it if anyone can, and I know that David will help. It's the worst thing I've ever encountered, and if you will get her out of there, I'll take full responsibility for her."

George's voice was low, and Sarah had to lean into the door to hear his answer. "I'll look into it tomorrow, Hettie, even though it's not in my line of expertise exactly. I'll see what can be done."

Hettie waited a moment and turned to leave the room. Sarah almost fell trying to get down the hall before Hettie came out. She was bursting with curiosity and could hardly wait to see if Hettie would confide in her. Her first thought was that Hettie was confronting George about what she and Hettie had talked about. She was relieved that was not the case, and she left her door open, hoping Hettie would come in and talk . She walked to her door and saw the older woman going in her own room.

The next morning, Hettie left the house before breakfast and did not return until noon. Sarah met her in the front hall and stopped her.

"Hettie, what in the world is going on? You look like someone chased you around the block." Hettie called her into her room and told her to sit down.

"Yesterday, Myrtle and I were going to a plant farm down toward Yacoma Creek, and we had car trouble. We walked down the road and saw a house down a narrow path, and we walked down and saw the door slightly ajar like someone was home. We hoped we could at least get a message back to town for some help. The woman that came to the door was no help, but she finally said she would send her little girl down the road and get a man that lived there to come - -that he was pretty good at fixing things, We waited on the porch, and I saw the little girl slipping out the back and going down the road. She was small, and of all things, seemed to be afraid for us to see her. The woman had disappeared in the house, so Myrtle and I just sat there on the ledge of the porch. In about 30 minutes or more, an old truck drove up with this man and no little girl. He seemed to know what to do, and I walked out to the car to watch and to ask him where the little girl was. He said she was walking back as her Mother didn't allow her to talk to anyone, so, she wouldn't get in the truck. Right before he got the car started and I paid him, I saw her going around the side of the house. I ran to meet her. She was afraid of me. Can you imagine anyone being afraid of me? I almost had to hold her to thank her and offer her a couple of dollars. She wasn't dirty, just neglected looking and scared out of her wits. She had on a pair of shoes that were a size too big. I asked her if she was supposed to be in school.

And she shook her head "No." She darted past me to the back door, and I followed her to insist she take the money."

"Please, Lady, don't follow me. Maw won't like it."

Hettie continued: "That little girl looked beyond into the house with such fear that I was determined to find out what in the world she was so afraid of and why she wouldn't ride back instead of that long walk. "What's your name? Mine's Hettie. Why can't you talk to me?" I pressed the money into her hand. I was horrified to see a long, red scar on the child's left arm. "Are you O.K. here? Do you need some help in some way? You are how old, dear?"

"The girl's eyes grew wild, and I looked around to see the woman standing behind me, and beckoning to the child, who ducked past me and disappeared into the house. I asked the woman if I could come back to see the child and what her name was—that I was certainly obligated to both of them. She gave me the name of "Bishop" and almost slammed the door in my face. Sarah, there is something terribly wrong at that house, and I intend to find out what it is." Hettie got her handkerchief out of her bosom and blew her nose.

That evening she met George at the door. "Did you get some kind of warrant or something so we can go out there and see what is wrong in that dreadful house?" Hettie was usually very reluctant to confront her big nephew this way, but she was determined to see the little girl again.

"Aunt Hettie, I talked with the Sheriff, and he says you will have to swear out a warrant to get in that place. Are you willing to do that? Of course, I'll back you up in whatever you do, so go down and see Wally tomorrow and do whatever you two can work out ." George walked on into his room and on into his bathroom. Hettie hardly slept a wink that night, and at 8 o'clock the next morning she was at the Sheriff's office. That afternoon she and Sheriff Jones drove up to the house, and the Sheriff turned to Hettie. "I didn't know anyone had moved into this old place." They walked to the door and knocked. It was some time before they saw the little girl staring at them from the ragged screen door. The Sheriff asked her if her Mother was home and she shook her head. She didn't come to the door but stood at a distance. Sheriff Jones opened the door, and when she saw Hettie she came forward and stood close to Hettie. Hettie put her arm around her, and as she did she saw the welts on her arms and legs.

"Sheriff, this child has been beaten - - look here." Wally Jones did look, and he told Hettie to take the girl to the car - - that she needed medical attention. They left a note on the kitchen table, that the child would be at the hospital in Oakville, and for Mrs. Bishop to come into town as soon as possible. Hettie sat as close to the frail child as she could, talking softly to her all the way. The next day charges of neglect and cruelty were filed against Mrs. Bishop. When Wally went out to serve the warrant, the house was empty. No one ever saw Mrs. Bishop again.

Nellie Thompson healed physically, but it was a long time before she healed emotionally. She was silent for three or four weeks but finally talked to Hettie about her life, which Hettie called "hell." The woman at the house was not her mother—she had been given to the woman nearly three years before. Mrs. Bishop had a business with men coming to the house, and Nellie was to clean and do the housework as payment for her keep. If she talked to anyone coming to the house she was beaten with a leather strap and refused food for that day. Also, since she had turned twelve, she was to substitute for "Miz Bishop" with the men who came when Miz Bishop was too busy, she said. The man who came to fix the car was one of her customers. Nellie had run away once, but Miz Bishop found her. Nellie almost died from the beating and wished she had. Now, she had her own room and new clothes and was registered for school. The doctor did what he could for the many scars she carried, and Hettie, Sarah, David and even George had only smiles for her; and the emotional scars were healing. She still did not sleep well, but she began to gain weight and was fast becoming an attractive young woman as Hettie's adopted daughter. She and Sarah became fast friends. Wally Jones's son, Paul, took her to the school parties and from then on Nellie was happy as anyone could be even with the memories she had to carry with her.

Chapter 19

Hettie and Nellie were shelling peas on the back porch, and the breeze was just cool enough to be comfortable. September was usually warmer than this year, and the cool breeze was a relief from the heat of the day before. Nellie looked at Hettie with open affection and poured her peas into the big bowl Hettie had in her lap.

"Aunt Hettie, I've so often wondered why you never married. You are so wonderful that any man would be lucky to have you. You're still pretty, and I know Mr. Jenkins just needs a little encouragement." Nellie looked at her friend with such love that Hettie reached over and hugged her, almost spilling the peas.

I guess I've never gotten over Joe Baumstein. Joe was the only son of a Jewish couple who were as orthodox as a Jewish family could be and did not believe in marrying outside the faith. They had already picked out a nice Jewish girl for him to marry. To marry me was out of the question, and they would never have accepted me. We slipped around for over two years, and I loved him so much and he loved me—of that I am sure."But"—and Hettie turned away –"he could not go against his parents, and he married the girl they chose. I was in my early thirties then, and I've never loved anyone since. I guess I'm a Parkes for sure. We're all kinda strange." She laughed softly. Nellie took the bowl of peas and kissed Hettie's cheek. "You're wonderful, Aunt Hettie. I hope they were all miserable."

Sarah was in the kitchen making an apple pie and heard most of the conversation on the porch. The story was now complete, as she has heard snatches of conversation about Joe, but she had never heard it all before. We are all kinda strange she thought. I guess I married into the right family. Nellie has a lot more gumption than I have. She asks questions and gets answers. I almost wish she would corner George for me sometime.

The little apple tree in the side yard had been full of apples this year, and she had put several pints in the freezer. George and David loved apple pie with ice cream. That was one thing she could count on that George would eat. She and Hettie would often ask him what he wanted to eat for supper, but he would say anything would be fine. David loved baked apples with pork chops, so he would get a double dose of apples that night, She had counted on the fresh peas that Hettie and Nellie would bring in, and that would be supper with biscuits and iced tea.

The two came in off the porch and set the peas down for her. She washed them and put them on to cook. The three women went into the den and sat together, friendly and easy with each other. Although Nellie was still young in years, she was accepted by both of them as their counterpart. Nellie was not quite a woman yet, but Sarah and Hettie considered her as wise and mature as anyone could be. Nellie had beautiful green eyes and shiny corn silk hair. She was growing into a really lovely looking young woman; she had been seeing two young guys in town, but it was Paul Jones who lighted up her countenance when he called or came by. Nellie could think of nothing in the world that would be better than being Mrs. Paul Jones. The phone rang at that moment, and Sarah and Hettie smiled as they heard her happy voice.

"It must be Paul." Hettie said.

Chapter 20

George Parkes had made a staunch friend in, of all places, New York City. His first flight up, he caught a cab at the Airport and gave the name of the hotel where he had made reservations for four nights. He was sitting quietly in the back seat, when he noticed the cab driver watching him in the rearview mirror. He remembered the warnings people had given him about how Yankees disliked southerners, so he looked out the window and said nothing The cab driver finally said: "I bet you are from the South." George smiled and answered him in his best southern drawl: " I sure am."

"Well, Sir, my name is O'Neal and welcome to New York." George thanked him, and again turned to the window.

"I have always wanted to move south, but my wife doesn't want to leave her family. I would like to live where it's warm most of the time and people are friendly." O'Neal continued to talk, and soon George began to respond. It took almost an hour to reach the hotel, and O'Neal jumped out, got George's bag and carried it into the hotel lobby. They shook hands, and O'Neal returned to his cab with a fare and a very large tip. He also returned with a very good feeling about southerners.

After the Bank Board Meeting the next day, George decided to take the ship to Staten Island, and he enjoyed the day. His other appointments were for the next day, and he had an eight o'clock dinner engagement that night with the Senior Vice President of the bank. He and his wife were having people in for dinner to meet their new Board member. It was getting dark when he left the ship, and he began to try to hail a cab. He was too slow and too cautious and every cab was taken before he could hail one down.

He began to get worried and was standing there almost alone when he heard someone calling to him from across the street.

"Mr. Parkes, you need a ride?" George saw a man with a woman and three children across the street. It was O'Neal with his family, and they were getting into his cab. O'Neal came across the street and shook his hand. "Come on, I'll take you to your hotel. All the cabs are gone, and I want you to meet my family." George Parkes left New York with a friend and a new regard for New Yorkers. Their friendship was to last; in fact, O'Neal was to be available in the future when George needed a cab and a friend. George made the dinner party on time, and was the center of attention, especially with a young M.D. named Adele Kessler. It was only a short time after he arrived in New York on his next trip that he was leaving the Hartwin Offices, that he was confronted by a very attractive young woman. It took him a minute to recognize Adele Kessler from the dinner party on his last trip.

George Parkes, I'm Adele Kessler, and I've been looking forward to seeing you again. We don't see many handsome southerners around here, and I wonder if you are available for the evening?" George was a little taken aback, but he smiled and managed to say' "Are you a friend of the Murdocks?"

"Yes, I am, and he told me you are alone up here and probably needing some company. I'm having a small group for dinner this evening, and I want you to come. Jasper and his wife will be there, and, oh, yes, I've got a cook from Alabama who cooks the best fried chicken you ever ate." She fairly glowed as she faced him, and he accepted before he thought twice.

Adele was smitten, and she was evident wherever George went while in New York. She made trips to the bank, and on his many appointments with Jasper Murdock, she was usually close by.

One evening she showed up at his hotel door, wine in hand, and completely at ease walked past him into his hotel room.

"You won't come to me, so I've come to you," she said. She slung her fur on the chair and turned to him. "George Parkes, you are the handsomest, most charming, most beautiful man I have ever met, and I intend for you to make love to me." She put her head on his chest and her arms went around his waist. When she looked up, he was not smiling and not receptive.

"Adele, you know full well what you are doing even if you have had too much to drink. You know that I am married and uninterested in any woman other than the one I have in Oakville, Mississippi, living in my house, carrying my name and my heart." Adele attempted to put her arms around his neck, but he caught them and pushed her away.

"You and I can be friends if you will put your coat on and leave. And take your wine." George grabbed her fur and put it and the wine in her hands.

O.K., you big stinker. I had to get pretty drunk to get up the nerve to do this. Just kiss me one time and I'll leave."

George propelled her to the door. As he did, she turned and kissed him full on the mouth. "You so-called southern gentlemen are damned fools," she said, as she stumbled out of the room.

Chapter 21

*H*ettie came home excited with news for Sarah. They were going to China! A group at the church were flying to Taipei, Taiwan, on the 15th, to visit Christ's College in Taipei, and Hettie had made up her mind that she would get George's permission for Sarah to join her. Not only did Sarah need to get away, but Hettie felt a strange longing to see another part of the world. She had never traveled to any extent, and this trip was exactly right for both of them. Nellie was old enough to stay home, and Betty would come in to keep the house for the boys, she thought. It was perfect, and Sarah soon responded to her with enthusiasm. George was agreeable, and they were at the airport in Memphis with the eighteen others who were as excited as they were. The flight was long with stay-over in Tokyo after leaving Dallas.

Taipei was the busiest place Hettie had ever seen, and Sarah felt breathless as they checked in at the beautiful hotel. The tour had requested reservations at the Grand Hotel, but there were no vacancies. Every day was busy with sightseeing and food and laughter. They were to spend two days at Christ's College. The day prior to that, they planned to spend the day at the Grand Hotel, and Hettie, Sarah, Dorothy and Miriam took a cab to the Hotel. The cab was old and creaky, and the driver was young and friendly. He smiled constantly and drove as fast as the old cab would go. He also had the radio on full-blast, and the wind through the open windows eliminated any chance of conversation. They paid him a dollar each, and he bowed and bowed again.

The hotel was no disappointment. The Lobby was enormous, and beautiful flowers and Oriental art were everywhere. Hettie had made a point to read about Christ's College before they had left home, and she had hopes of at least getting to see Dr, Graham who was the founder after leaving Red China with Chang Kaichek. Chang had brought many treasures with him acquired while he was in power on the Mainland. The Museum near the Grand Hotel was fabulous. The three older women went to the Rest Room, and Sarah sat in an elegant carved chair to watch the people and see the beautiful surroundings. She had put on her dark glasses in the cab and had not removed them when five uniformed Chinese men walked in. The one who seemed to be in charge saw her, walked straight over to her and bowed. Sarah was too surprised to turn away, and she extended her hand which he took and kissed it. As he bowed before her, his medals hung below in such numbers that she realized he must be someone in power. The other four officers stood back and watched silently. The Officer said something to her in Chinese, and she shook he head and smiled again. He held her hand a moment longer then turned and walked away. The three women had returned in time to see what had happened. Sarah was to be reminded many times how she had captivated one of the rulers of Taipei in the Grand Hotel on the island of Taiwan. The stories they told of Christ College and how American missionaries joined Dr. Graham to teach the

English language to the eager, young Chinese students, along with the language studies the Christian Bible with no interference from the Taiwanese government.

The four of them walked the halls of the fabulous Hotel, finding numerous shops and eating places. Hettie stopped suddenly at one restaurant and walked to a table where an enormous American sat waiting for his food. She left the other three dumbfounded at the entrance.

"Dr, Graham?" she asked. The portly gentleman rose from his chair and offered her his hand. They talked a minute, and he motioned to the other three to join them. He was delighted to have them join him for lunch which he ordered for all of them in fluent Mandarin and insisted on paying for all of them. Needless to say, this time with this great man was the highlight of their trip. Dr. Graham spent his life in China and died there many years later. His enormous physical size fit well with the enormous legacy he left in the country he adopted as his own. Hettie and Sarah often sat for long periods of time remembering their trip. When first Hettie related the incident in the Grand Hotel and the Chinese official approaching Sarah, George silenced her with a glance.

"Hettie," and he did not smile as he said it, "if you had let anything happen to Sarah, you would have had to stay over there." Sarah looked at her husband with greater feeling than she had felt in a long time. He does love me, she thought.

Chapter 22

*D*avid had thought about his situation at home, and now that he and George had finally been able to talk fully, he felt a need to do something about his lack of seeking female companionship outside his own house. He owed George that. Being in a wheelchair and having to have help to go anywhere other than the bank and home, he usually did just that – the bank and home. Pepper Lucas was nearly always available and even anxious to go with him, to drive and to help with the chair. It was difficult to take a date out and to have help to get in a café or movie or party. He sometimes declined invitations to social affairs, but there was one the next weekend he wanted to attend. Lelia Garrett had been friendly to the point of seeking him out at the bank, and he felt sure she would like to go. That evening he called her, and she seemed really glad to hear from him. He told Pepper he needed him for the evening, and Pepper badly needed the money. He also loved to drive that big black car, and he told David: "Yes, sir, Mr. Parkes, I'll be there at seven sharp. Yes sir."

They picked Lelia up with Pepper calling for her at the door. She was dressed in a lovely green silk suit, and her red hair glistened in the light of the car. She got in as Pepper opened the door and sat over close to David in the back seat. "I thought you would never call me, David," she said. He smiled and told Pepper to take them to the reception at the University - - Dr. Green's residence. He and Lelia talked easily, Lelia leaning into him all the way. David decided she needed no encouragement, but later he would see how far she would go. Pepper's presence in the front seat did not seem to bother her at all. Pepper got them to the party with no trouble at all, and David rolled easily beside Lelia as they made the rounds and sipped the beverage they were served. It was an hour later and Lelia had enjoyed several drinks, when David decided it was time to leave. Pepper was waiting at the door. David could not decide if Lelia had had too much champagne or if she was always this way. She sat so close to him that he almost had to push her away, and without any prompting she caught his face and pulled him to her, kissing him passionately on the mouth. David kissed her back, but she would not let him pull away from her when he decided he did not want this to go any farther. As soon as he could get far enough away from her, he told Pepper to take them home. Lelia was furious.

"David Parkes, you know I've waited for you a very long time. We're together at last, and I don't want to go home."

"I'm sorry, Lelia, but I have to limit my time out. I'll try to call you again soon." David smiled and caught Pepper's eye in the mirror.

Pepper had stopped at her house, and he got out and opened the back door for her. She looked like she could kill him, and slammed her door when she went in. Pepper walked slowly back to the car.

"Wow, Mr. Parkes," he said, getting back in the car, "That lady is no lady," They both laughed.

Chapter 23

*N*ellie had bloomed in the time that she had been with Hettie, Sarah, David and George - - Betty also had become her close friend; and the two of them often sat at the kitchen table and talked about their ups and downs. Nellie had fewer downs these days than Betty it seemed, and when Nellie thought about it after their frank discussions, she realized that Betty's husband did not work much and left home frequently. Nellie hoped and prayed that Paul would love her and their home, and she felt that she had little to worry about in that area. She and Paul had set the date of June 7th, and Hettie was making her wedding dress, Sarah was providing the veil, the shoes and the flowers. David and George were providing the food and the cost of the reception. Nellie was in high heaven and could hardly wait for the time when she and Paul would be together. She wanted him, his name and she wanted his children. They had waited for their wedding night for the consummation of their marriage, and Nellie loved him even more for being patient with her. She and Sarah had agreed on a small bouquet of orchids for her, and Sarah was to be her Matron-of-Honor. George would be there to give her away, and Hettie would serve as her Maid-of-Honor. There was an open invitation to the wedding, and after a beautiful ceremony and reception, they went to the mountains for a week's honeymoon. When they returned, Nellie was pregnant and as happy as anyone could be. Nine months later she gave birth to a nine pound baby boy, and they discussed naming him "Paul Parkes Jones."

When Paul thought about it, he quickly said that would not do. He said he would never submit to his son being named "P. P. Jones".

"I know how kids think," he said. "It wouldn't take long for those P"s to have double ee's on the end of them." So, Nellie and Paul named their son "Paul Latham Jones."

Not many times had George Latham shown such pride, and Paul Latham Jones would be very special to him. George Latham felt as though he finally had an heir of sorts and one he was very proud of. Little Paul Latham was mentioned more than once in the Will that George Latham wrote before he died.

Chapter 24

*I*t was a bright sunny day, and Nellie was hanging diapers on the line in the backyard. Paul Latham was in his buggy close by in the shade, and both seemed happy with the world. A sound behind Nellie startled her, and she turned quickly to face a small, skinny little woman with a wrinkled but pleasant face.

"You have a fine looking boy there" the woman said. "I bet he is a healthy young'n. Many a time I wished I had me a son." She seemed to be groping for words. "I have been living in Hot Coffee, and Dr. Russ told me you might need some help what with you helping in the Sheriff's office. I sure do need a job, and I will work for my keep. Dr. Russ can tell you I am clean and honest and I truly love babies." She looked down at her feet. Nellie did too and saw she badly needed some shoes. Those she wore were threadbare, and the woman shuffled her feet trying to hide the ill-fitting shoes. Her feet were misshapen.

"Oh, by the way, Miz Jones, my name is Pearl Ramsey, and I sure hope you will let me work for you."

Nellie looked away and thought about the situation and

wondered what Paul would say. She told the woman to come in the back door with her, she picked up the baby and they went in the kitchen. Nellie had made some cupcakes that morning and offered the woman one and a cup of coffee. She sat down and watched her eat. She seemed famished.

"I'll call my husband, and you know he will have to check with Dr. Russ. I do need some help."

"Yes, Ma'am, I know. I surely hope you can use me. I will not only keep your baby, but I will cook and iron and do whatever is needed. All I need is a bed and a drawer to put my things in. I don't have much." Pearl Ramsey was almost pleading. Nellie was almost sure that Pearl had no place to go. Later when Paul called Dr. Russ, he found out that the good doctor had sold his place and that he had retired and was to move to Chicago to live with his son. He had called Jake Smith and Jake and told him to contact the Sheriff in Oakville.

Pearl moved in with Nellie and her family. Her whole attitude was humble and self-effacing, and she soon became a needed and loved part of the family.

It was not but a few days into Pearl's second month with the Jones family that Nellie was putting up clothes in the big chifferobe that she noticed an apron of Pearl's in her personal laundry, and she went in Pearl's room and opened the door to place the apron when she noticed a framed picture of a woman and a small girl. Nellie nearly fainted, as she saw herself with a much younger, pretty Pearl Ramsey.

"Pearl is my mother," she murmured. She sat on the side of the bed. "She's known it all along. Little Paul is her grandson. Dear Lord, what am I to do?" She decided to wait until she had calmed down a little before she called Paul and let him help her decide how to face Pearl. All she knew was that God does work in mysterious ways.

That evening after Paul and Paul Latham had gone to sleep, she went to Pearl's room. She knocked and found her Mother sitting in the rocking chair by the window. She opened her mouth to speak but Pearl spoke first.

"Nellie, I have not been honest with you. I have been so afraid that you would throw me out if I told you - - Nellie, I only gave you away because I could not feed and clothe you. Your father and I were married, but he walked off and left me. I never went to school until I began to work for Dr. Russ. You have helped me so much with my read'n and write'n. I will never make it up to you, but truly, Nellie, I love you and I loved you then." She walked over to her daughter with tears streaming down her face. Nellie put her arms around the frail little woman who had given her life, and they held each other for several minutes.

Together they walked to Paul Latham's room, and walked over to his bed. He awoke and Nellie turned the bedside light on. The little boy stood in his bed and grabbed the side rail and grinned from ear to ear, and his two front teeth glistened in the light. All three of them, for some reason, started laughing. Only Paul Latham, little as he was, seemed to know the reason why.

Chapter 25

The big car was in its place early that morning, a full hour before the bank would open; and George Parkes sat at his desk facing the shiny surface that Katie Farr, his secretary had cleared off the night before after he left. He looked at his hands which were shaking slightly and he grimaced as he put his arms down on the desk. He thought of his Uncle Latham and his brother, David, and he tried very hard not to think of his Sarah. What kind of man am I he thought? I married a beautiful, wonderful woman half my age, and I have never been able to make her happy. I know she cares about me, and she is the only woman I have ever loved. God forgive me!

He sat there a long time and began to hear the employees coming in the front, and he turned to the window. He did not want to see anyone right now and knew Katie would not bother him if he faced the window. That was his time alone, and she honored it. When she knocked and opened the door, he was facing the door again and told her to let Don Packer in when he came.

"I am giving him some time on his mortgage," he told Katie. "They have just had another baby, and he will need some time to catch up. Go ahead and draw up the papers and I will stay here until I see him; then I am going home. Don't feel so well this morning."

Katie looked at him with an openness that she had never displayed before. She wanted to put her arms around him and comfort him but she could not. George Parkes was, and she tried to think of the proper word, "inaccessible".

Don Packer arrived right on time and left with a new feeling of hope and determination to pay the bank as soon as possible. He had always had a deep respect for George Parkes, and his whole demeanor improved as he left the bank.

George had added a small bathroom to his private office. No one used that bathroom except he, not even David. George went in and opened the cabinet above the sink and got two pills out of a prescription bottle. It had Dr. Murdock's name on it. He had refilled it the last time he was in New York. He took the pills with a glass of water, locked the door of the cabinet and returned to his office, carefully closing the bathroom door. He put on his hat and walked into the outer area. All the employees were busy setting up for the day.

As he walked to the door to leave, all eyes were on him, and he straightened up when he heard Katie say;

"Take care, Mr. Parkes."

He turned and looked back, his eyes covering the whole big room. He smiled and half-waved, as he went out the door. Katie's eyes filled with tears.

"Dear Lord," she whispered to herself. "How I love that man!"

Chapter 26

Things began to change in the Parkes' house, and Sarah was to learn of George's reasons for his reluctance to be with her. George was in pain at times and began to stay at home. His trips to New York had stopped, and he only went to the bank a time or two a week. David had taken over his duties and was far more accessible than his brother. He urged George to talk to Sarah, and George said he would. Time passed and even Hettie worried openly about the change in her nephew's appearance. He was almost frail looking and ate very little. She asked him many times what was wrong, but he refused to tell her.

Finally Sarah went in his room where he stayed most of the time with his books and radio and sat down on the chaise with him and told him she had waited a long time, that she knew something was wrong - - that she deserved to know. She looked into his eyes, and he looked back at her for the first time in a long time. His eyes were bright and feverish looking, and she felt a pang in her very being. Now she realized what pain he was in. Sarah was not an obtuse woman. She had grown up in a family of five children without a Mother, and being the youngest girl, she had learned that silence was her best weapon. She had been well all her life, and she had little understanding of how to deal with sickness. Somehow, she had refused or was unable to realize how close she was to losing this man she loved but hardly knew. Sarah had always had difficulty dealing with reality if it made her uncomfortable. That was how she had dealt with George's seeming indifference toward her all these years. It was almost that if she didn't dwell on it, it would get better - - that all she had to do was wait. Even now she refused to get to the core of their problem. She simply didn't want to deal with it.

George had always seemed to realize this, and he dealt with it in the only way he knew how. He believed in himself as being able to overcome anything in his own strength and in his own way. He lay there and looked into her eyes without saying a word, and it was that look that Sarah carried to her grave. He didn't want her sympathy or her pity, but he did want her love. She knew then that George had always needed her. When she leaned over closer to his face, he caught her hand and kissed it. The light left his eyes and he died holding her hand. Sarah had never witnessed death before.

Sarah did not call anyone for a long time. She sat there with her hand in his, choked with emotion. It was much later when Hettie called through the door saying Dr. Baker was there to see George. Sarah went to the door and went to the porch without saying a word. She sat down on the front steps and the flood of tears came. Hettie had gone to George's room with Dr. Baker, and Sarah had the time she needed to be alone. Never before had she felt completely desolate. Almost numb. Finally, she could deal with her marriage to George. She was more at fault than he was. She realized her seeming indifference was what this proud and sensitive man, her husband, could not handle. It would never leave her that she had failed him far more than he had failed her.

Summer came and went and five months later, David asked her to marry him. They waited until almost Christmas and were married in the Church office with only a few guests standing with Nellie, Paul and Hettie. David had planned a cruise for their honeymoon, but Sarah told him to cancel it, that she just wanted to go to New Orleans for a few days and that she could drive. The days flew by, and Sarah felt a real peace for the first time since George's death. She could almost feel his blessing.

Dr. Baker had explained to Sarah that George had cancer and had been going to a clinic in New York for treatments and testicular surgery for a very long time. He wanted to go into detail but David had asked him not to, that Sarah knew enough now and that she didn't handle that sort of thing too well. Dr. Baker obliged. Sarah did not admit even to herself until she was older that she was not and never had been the woman she had always thought she was—that her attitude toward illness and pain was shallow and even unkind. In the months following George's death she often sat with Mariah on the back porch watching the birds and squirrels and wishing she had been far more helpful and much wiser in helping a husband who needed her. She now had a full life with David and their son, and a handsome David Latham he was. She adored him and thanked God every day for him.

As Sarah thought about it, she remembered how long she had waited for George to really show his love for her in the way she needed. She closed her eyes and felt the peace in her heart and knew that her season of fulfillment had been worth the waiting. She knew full well that she had a lot of regrets along with her memories and that the tears were still ready to spill over. She put her blue nightgown on and waited for David to join her in bed. The tears would have to wait for another time.

Chapter 27

George's death left Sarah with a need for something worthwhile to do with her time. She stayed in her room for several days after the funeral. She didn't even want to see Hettie. She realized how much George had meant to the people in Oakville. Everyone in town came to the funeral service, and there were many who could not get in the funeral home and later at the church. There were many people standing around the church, and the food brought to the house would feed them for days. She had asked for no flowers, but the room where the casket stood was full of beautiful sprays and stands of flowers. George Parkes had helped so many people in his quiet, unobtrusive way that Sarah was amazed. It made her remember her seeming lack of comfort to him even more, and she decided that definitely she would try to live up to being Mrs. George Latham Parkes.

Sarah called Dr. Baker a month after George's death, and she asked him if there was a volunteer service she could join. He told her there was a Home for Old Men about seven miles out of town that few people knew about, and he said they could use any kind of help they could get. He also told her that they needed money, food and personal service of any kind. Sarah got directions and drove out to The Home the next morning. It was a big, ugly old house but with a huge yard filled with beautiful shade trees and a big front porch filled with rocking chairs. A friendly reddish-colored dog met her car out front, and she greeted the dog and was welcomed with a dignified bark. She and Lady became fast friends.

The man who met her in the front foyer was tall with a short trim beard. He was glad to see her and said he knew who she was—George Parkes' wife. Like most, he spoke George's name with respect. George had helped them many times with funds to cover emergencies.

The man at the door introduced himself as Ralph Davis, and he took her back to his small office. Two days later, Sarah was busy in the Recreation Room, helping with wheelchairs, passing out water and juice and serving cookies which she brought each time she came.

It was difficult not to show partiality. Some of the men were totally unaware of their surroundings, some were not mentally alert and many were blind, deaf and unable to converse at all. Sarah tried very hard to talk to each one no matter how unresponsive they were, and she always tried to correct anything she saw that was wrong. Sarah often made one or more much more comfortable by getting something needed or just sitting and talking or reading to one or another.

Sarah had been coming to The Home twice a week for several months and had become fond of most of the old men she worked with and attended. One of the oldest patients, Mr. Sainter, had a daughter living five miles away. She came to see her father a time or two a month. Sarah began to try to spend special time with him because no one else did. He was a fine looking 90 years old, white hair and still fairly alert and always shaved and clean looking. He began to look for her on her regular days with Lady by his side. She always spent as much time with them as she could.

On one of her visits, she saw him over in the corner with his head low on his chest and not even aware she was there. Lady lay by his side and did not even look up. She joined them.

"Hi, Mr. Sainter," and she patted him on the shoulder. "How are you today?" I brought some cookies, your favorite kind," he looked up at her, and he had a big blue streak across his left cheek, and his lip had been bleeding.

"What in the world happened to you, Mr. S.?" she asked him. He didn't answer, and his eyes filled with tears. Sarah pulled up a chair and sat down by him. Lady moved up closer as if waiting for the answer. Sarah patted his hand and noticed a black and blue welt on it. It was evident something bad had happened to him, and he didn't feel like talking about it. Sarah was determined to find out what had happened to him, and she sat there close to him. He finally looked up at her, and she smiled and continued to talk to him.

"My roommate beat me with his cane," he said. His voice quivered so that she could hardly understand him. "He's done it before, but this time he really hurt me."

Sarah was horrified. She took him in his wheelchair to the small office. Mr. Davis was on the phone but finished and turned to her.

"Look at this, Mr. Davis," Sarah said, her voice very emotional. "That man you put in Mr. Sainter's room is mean, and I told you that a month ago. He has beaten Mr. Sainter for the last time. I don't intend to leave here until you have him out of Mr. Sainter's room. He's dangerous!"

Ralph Davis looked at the black and blue places on Sainter's arms and face, and he got up, went down the hall and entered the room where the two old men lived. He pulled the other man's clothes out of the closet, put them in his lap and pushed the surprised old man out of the room and down the hall.

That night Mr. Sainter slept well for the first time in a long time. His ex-roommate slept in the storeroom next to the kitchen. The next day he joined another curmudgeon who lived at the back of the hall. If he ever beat on that roommate, he probably received back blow for blow.

Sarah's affection for Mr. S. probably helped him stay in the land of the living for almost another year, as he often told her how much he loved her. He said he would ask her to marry him if he weren't so old. She was with him the day he died at 93 years old. The year before the doctor had given him three months to live.

When her circumstances changed drastically, Sarah sent a check every month as long as The Home remained open. Ralph Davis moved to another nursing home with private patients. The patients in The Home were placed in other facilities. Sarah never forgot Mr. Sainter and smiled each time she thought of his wanting to marry her. The best thing about me, she told Hettie, older men really love me - - wonderful, older men. No woman could ever wish for anything better!

Chapter 28

The summer that George Parkes died was a summer that another major event occurred in Oakville. Not only did it lose its most outstanding citizen and banker, but another incident "caught the breeze" and kept everyone aware of something besides the weather—which ranged anywhere from 95 to 105 degrees.

Every child in Oakville knew the Whisker Man and were afraid of him. They had been accustomed to being warned: "If you don't behave, I'll give you to the Whisker Man." That was his name, and he seemed to like it. He pushed a cart around with a big, wide broom; and he kept the streets of Oakville clean of litter. Someone hired him and someone paid him a small fee, but few knew where he lived or what his real name was.

Whisker Man had a long, smooth beard that fell to his waist. It was not bristly as most beards are but lay flat against his chest and was the color of suet, as was his hair down his back. He wore a dark shirt, open at the neck and a pair of non-descript trousers with a rope for a belt. His shoes were always untied and did not seem to fit. He shuffled along and seldom looked up. When he did, his eyes were almost slits and he never spoke to anyone. He pushed his cart and picked up the litter and kept Oakville clean.

One morning right before noon, he was seen to go in the jail by the Sheriff, who followed him in. Wally was puzzled as to why Whiskers would visit the jail. He never had before.

Whiskers was sitting on the bench inside the door, and Wally Jones could not believe his eyes. The top of Jess Denner's small body showed in his push cart, and blood covered the side of his head. "He was bothering a little girl, and he ran from me and fell and hit his head. I told him not to do it again, but he did. I would'da hit him, and he knew it 'cause I had told him before." Jeff Denner was dead.

As it turned out, Whiskers was exonerated. Wally Jones was his best witness, and Denner's daughter did not contest the case. Thomas Kite saw Whiskers walking east out of town early one morning, soon after the trial. Oakville was never the same. There was much talk that summer about the whole business, but Hettie said it best: "The kids were always scared of the wrong man." She looked a little sheepish. "I guess I was too!"

Epilog

Sarah sat in the swing, slowly pushing with one foot and enjoying the slight motion. A soft breeze was blowing, and her favorite oak trees were gently swaying. She always thought of the larger one as the male and the smaller, fuller branched one as the female. They just look that way to me, she thought. Her big dog, Boomer, sat close by on the small green rug, and he would look around at her and wag his tail. He doesn't look a thing like Mariah, she thought, but he's just as sweet as she was.

"Lord have mercy," she whispered, "I'm almost 80 years old, and Boomer and I are all alone, and he's almost as old as I am. Where have the years gone? I even think of Tad Parkes sometimes." She laughed. "I'm his Great Aunt or his cousin-in-law or something. I even got real excited over him once a long time ago. He was the first Parkes in my life."

Sarah looked at her hands covered with brown spots and so wrinkled. She could almost see her hands when she was young, and she remembered how soft and white and graceful they were.

"Boomer, sometimes when I look in the mirror I want to cry because I have changed so much, and yet, so many tell me I haven't changed at all. Kay Toler knew me the other day, and I hadn't seen her in thirty years and I didn't recognize her. I'm grateful I've lived this long, but I wish I looked more like I did for David and George. Most of my friends are dead or in retirement homes. I'm going to stay in this big house where all my precious memories are as long as I *can. I can still get out in the car and I can still take care of myself. And you, Boomer, can still bark and look vicious on occasion. I haven't figured out yet whether I've become wise or not. Certainly, wisdom should come when you've lived as long as I have."*

She looked out across the lawn. "I've thought about Jean a lot lately. I will always remember her. She should have married Fred like everybody thought she would instead of running off with that high falutin' Captain from New Jersey. She wrote for awhile and then just quit. Even her family never knew what happened to her or wouldn't tell. Life's not always fair, Boomer, as you and I know; but I guess God didn't promise that it would be. I've just always hoped nothing terrible happened to her.

"My family drifted apart after Dad died. I had always thought that Bo and l would end up together here in Oakville, but even he moved to Chicago with the Tribune. His wife still writes, but that's about all the family I have left—she and her kids—and I don't even know them. Evelyn lived in Hawaii until she and her husband died. I don't know her kids either. Richard's been gone a long time, and he is the one I feel the greatest loss over. He and I were alike in so many ways. Laney turned out to be real successful, married, and never had any children. Her car accident was the blow that finished Dad off, I believe. Oh, well, I bought a new suit yesterday, Boomer, and it's really good looking. I still have a waistline, and I love teaching my class at church. I'll see Nellie and her brood there Sunday. Thank goodness, they live close by."

She got up with her fingers touching Boomer's head. "I hope

David Latham calls me tonight. He keeps me young. That's right, Boomer, I said young. My son is my joy, and you, Boomer, are my best friend." She walked to her room and sat down at her dressing table. She took the cold cream and slowly covered her face, slowly rubbing it in. She cleaned it off with a Kleenex and put toothpaste on her toothbrush and brushed her teeth. Almost aloud, she thanked God that she still had all her teeth. She changed to her gown, turned the cover back and got in bed. Boomer watched carefully until she was settled and turned to switch the bedside lamp off. He jumped on the foot of the bed, and they settled down for the night.

Just then, the phone rang. She turned the lamp back on. "That's probably David Latham," she said as she answered.

"Well, for heaven's sake, Tad, I was just thinking about you. How's Oklahoma? She listened a moment, "Please do come, Tad, I'd love to see you." She laughed softly. "Oh, yes, Tad. You can stay as long as you like."

THE END

When you look back at life, it appears as a vapor, or so the sages say. To me, as I look back, that is not so---every minute of life lingers and stirs in my memory, full of color and time.

–MM